PONY CLUB
SECRETS

❧Comet❧
and the
Champion's Cup

The Pony Club Secrets series:

Also available

PONY CLUB
SECRETS

Comet
and the
Champion's Cup

Stacy Gregg

HarperCollins *Children's Books*

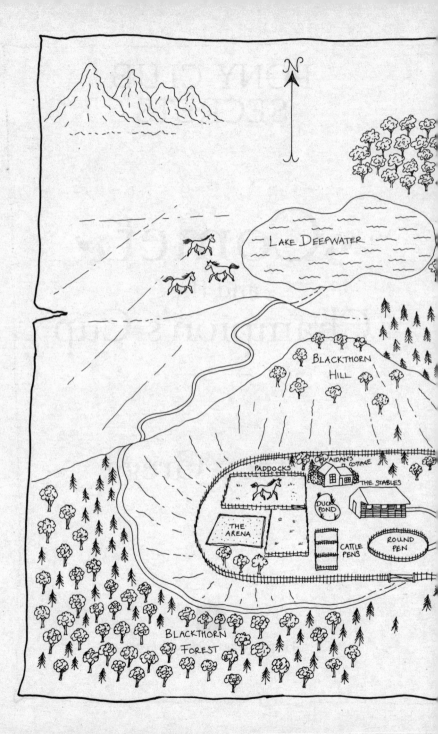

For Kirsty, who was there and
knows what really happened...

www.stacygregg.co.uk

First published in Great Britain by HarperCollins *Children's Books* in 2009.
HarperCollins *Children's Books* is a division of HarperCollins*Publishers* Ltd,
1 London Bridge Street, London SE1 9GH

This edition published in 2015

www.harpercollins.co.uk

16

Text copyright © Stacy Gregg 2008
Illustrations © Fiona Land 2008

ISBN-13 978-0-00-727030-9

The author and illustrator assert the moral right to be identified
as the author and illustrator of the work.

Printed and bound in England by CPI Group (UK) Ltd, Croydon CR0 4YY

MIX
Paper from
responsible sources

FSC C007454
www.fsc.org

CHAPTER 1

The bay colt knew the girl was watching. He arched his neck proudly, delighting in her attention as he trotted by. When he passed the paddock railing where the girl was sitting, the colt came so close that he almost brushed against her knees. She giggled and reached out a hand to grab him, but the colt swerved away, putting on a sudden burst of speed, galloping away from her to the other side of the paddock.

When he reached the hedge at the end of the field his flanks were heaving and his muzzle was twitching with excitement. He wheeled about, his ears pricked forward, turning to face the girl who stared intently back at him.

The girl whistled. Her lips pursed together as she blew once, then a second time – a sharp, clear note that carried across the paddock. The colt heard her call, but at first he refused to obey, stamping at the ground and tossing his head defiantly. He held his ground briefly, his muscles quivering, before he leapt forward as if he were a racehorse, breaking from the gate. Thrilling in his own speed as his eager strides swallowed up the ground between them, the colt galloped back to her, wanting to start the whole game again.

"Good boy, Storm!" Issie giggled as the colt swept past again, once more managing to avoid her hand as she reached out to touch him.

They had played this game of tig many times, but Issie never got tired of it. She loved to watch Nightstorm move. His body still hadn't grown into those long, lanky legs – it was as if he were teetering about on stilts – and yet there was something so graceful about him.

Nightstorm was hardly recognisable as the tiny bay foal with the white blaze that had been born that stormy night in the stables here at Winterflood Farm. It was Issie who had named the colt Nightstorm as they sheltered together in the stables while the lightning flashed above their heads. Lately, though, she had taken to calling him by his nickname – Storm.

Storm was just three months old, but already Issie

could see that he was the best possible combination of both of his magnificent bloodlines. His elegant head carriage and beautiful, dished Arabian face were derived from his Anglo-Arab dam, Blaze. Physically, though, the colt was much more solid than his mother. He bore a powerful resemblance to his sire, the great grey stallion Marius. You could see it in his well-rounded haunches, classical topline and strong, solid hocks, all true signs of the Lipizzaner breed.

As the colt cantered back once more, Issie leapt down off the rails, a signal that the game was over. Storm understood this. He trotted towards her and didn't try to swerve away this time. Instead, he came to a halt right next to her so that Issie could reach out and stroke his velvety muzzle. She ran her hand down the colt's neck. Storm was already moulting, losing the soft, downy layer of fur that all foals are born with, to reveal the shiny, smooth grown-up coat underneath. Issie could see bits of deep russet bay, the colour of warm mahogany, emerging from underneath the baby-fluff.

Storm was growing fast. Sometimes Issie felt it was too quick – she wanted him to be a foal forever. At other times, she felt it still wasn't fast enough. Horses take a long time to mature – and horses with Lipizzaner blood take longer than most. It would be three years before Storm was ready to be ridden. Such a long time! Issie had bitten her lip and tried not to say anything childish when Avery told her how long she must wait to ride the colt, but inside she felt bitterly disappointed. She didn't want to wait. She wanted to ride Storm now!

It had never occurred to Issie that when her beloved mare Blaze had a foal it would mean she would be left without a horse to ride for the whole of the summer holidays. She couldn't ride Storm – and Blaze couldn't be ridden yet either, not until the colt was weaned at six months. And that was ages away!

Never mind, Issie thought. She might not be able to ride, but she loved just being with her new baby. She was amazed at how quickly Storm seemed to put his trust in her. Perhaps it was because he had watched Issie and Blaze together and he was simply following his mother's cues. His mother was the centre of his universe and if his mum loved this girl with the long dark hair, well, then Storm loved her too. Issie could have happily spent her summer goofing around with the colt, playing silly games like the one they were playing today – if it weren't for Avery getting all serious on her.

"He's just a cute baby now," Avery pointed out.

"But that foal of yours will be a sixteen-two hands high stallion one day. He's getting stronger every day, bigger too. That's why it's important to start his schooling now, while he's still small enough for you to be able to handle him. It's important to teach Nightstorm good manners and respect right from the start."

And so, under Avery's expert tuition, Issie began learning how to "imprint" her foal. She followed her instructor's advice to the letter, being firm but gentle with Storm as she taught him to accept a head collar and then a foal halter, how to walk politely beside her on a lead rein and how to stand perfectly still while she picked up his feet.

Issie would arrive at Winterflood Farm at dawn most mornings so she could spend time with the colt before school. She would bring Storm and Blaze into the stable block and spend the next hour grooming the colt while the mare ate her hard feed. The grooming sessions were a gradual process, part of the colt's training, teaching him to accept her touch as she ran the brushes over his body. The whole time she worked, Issie would talk softly to Storm, and he would occasionally nicker back to her, turning around to snuffle her softly with his velvety muzzle when she was brushing him, or closing his eyes in pleasure as she scratched him on that sweet spot on his rump.

The weekends were the best. Then she would cycle down to Winterflood Farm at dawn and wouldn't return home until dinner time. Issie couldn't really say exactly what she did at the farm all day. Sometimes she just lay in the long grass under the magnolia tree and watched Storm. She especially loved the way he would snort and quiver each time something new crossed his path. She could hardly wait until next week when the school holidays would finally be starting and she could spend all her time with the young horse.

Today, Issie had another new surprise for the colt. As she reached into her pocket and produced a carrot, she watched Storm boggle at it with wide eyes. He hadn't learnt to eat carrots yet – and he was uncertain what to do next.

"Here you go, Storm," Issie said softly, extending her hand, the carrot in her palm. Storm had watched his mother eat carrots before, but he'd never been offered one to try himself. He gave it a sniff and his ears pricked forward. It smelt good! He gave Issie's palm a snuffle, taking a tiny little bite, then he held the chunk of carrot in his mouth, unsure of what to do next. Issie giggled again at the expression on his face, those wide dark brown eyes filled with wonder.

"Here, Blaze, you show him how it's done!" Issie grinned, giving one to the colt's mother as well. The mare took the carrot eagerly, crunching it down. Issie was about to dig another carrot out of her jacket pocket and try to feed Storm again when she heard her name being called.

"Issie!" She turned around to see Tom Avery standing on the back porch of the cottage. "Your mum is on the phone. She wants to talk to you."

Issie sighed. "She probably wants me to come home and tidy my room. She's been on at me about getting it done before the holidays begin."

Avery smiled at her. "It is possible that your mother just wants to lay eyes on you for five minutes to make sure you actually exist. You've been spending all your time here with Storm."

Issie paused on the back porch to yank off her boots before padding along the hallway to pick up the phone. "Hi, Mum," she said brightly. "Listen, if it's about my room, I know I said I'd tidy it, but I couldn't find the vacuum cleaner nozzle and…"

Her mother interrupted her. "I've just had a phone

call from Aidan." Mrs Brown's voice was taut and serious. "Issie, I'm afraid it's bad news. It's about your aunty Hess…"

Hester had woken at 3 a.m. and, finding herself wide awake, resigned herself to her fate. She switched on her bedside lamp and tried to occupy herself with a crossword puzzle, but found it impossible to concentrate on the page in front of her. Her eyes kept darting nervously away from the newspaper in her hand to her laptop, which sat silently in the dark on her desk. She was waiting for an important email and, until it arrived, sleep was out of the question.

At 6 a.m., as the light came streaming in through the wide bay windows of Blackthorn Manor, she finally heard the sound that she had been longing for and dreading at the same time: the soft "ping" that signalled that an email had arrived in her inbox. She walked across the room and looked at the screen. *You've got mail!* it flashed at her urgently.

Hester held her breath as she clicked the mouse to open the email. She was so sick with nerves, she could barely bring herself to look at it. *Please let it be good news,* she thought to herself. *We need this film so badly!*

From the very first line, though, her heart sank.

```
Dear Hester, it is with great regret
that we inform you that all work has been
delayed indefinitely on our latest film
project…
```

Hester didn't bother to read any further. She knew what the rest of the email said. And she knew exactly what it meant – total disaster. She shut the laptop immediately, as if closing it would keep the bad news locked inside where it couldn't upset her any more. She felt a sudden chill and wrapped her dressing gown tightly around herself as she left her bedroom and walked downstairs.

Padding down to the kitchen in silence with the dogs following at her feet, Hester put the kettle on and began to make coffee. She looked out of the window towards the stables. The horses would be waking up in their stalls and expecting their breakfast. They had no idea about the email – or the bad news it contained.

"Well, my Daredevil Ponies," Hester said darkly, "I'd like to see what stunt you can pull to get us out of this mess."

"Hester?"

Hester turned around to find her young stable manager Aidan standing in the doorway. Aidan looked like he hadn't slept either. He ran a hand through his hair, pushing back his long dark fringe to reveal striking blue eyes that were restless with the worry and stress they had both shared over the past few weeks.

"Has there been any news? Have you heard back from the production company yet?"

Hester nodded solemnly. "It's all bad I'm afraid. They've postponed the movie – indefinitely. We're out of work again. I just don't believe it. Three film jobs falling through in a row. We've got the luck of the devil hounding us, Aidan. I just wish we had his money too. I was relying on this movie. There's no way I can keep things going now…"

"Of course you can!" Aidan said. "Hester… I've been thinking about it and you don't have to pay me. I mean, I don't need much to live on and I've got my room and board here. You can forget about my salary until you've got some money again. I was thinking maybe we could do a deal with the feed and grain merchants too. I'm sure they'd help you out. If you just told them the situation, and we promised to pay again when things get better…"

Hester smiled back at Aidan. "That's very kind, dear, but feed merchants aren't very keen on charity. And in case you haven't noticed, it's already been over a month since I last paid you. I don't expect you to keep working for me for free." Hester looked at Aidan's forlorn expression. "I appreciate your offer, I really do. But even if I wasn't paying your salary, there's still the mortgage. And the maintenance. This place is so big and so old, it needs an enormous amount of money just to keep it running. And all the horses need shoeing and there are vet's bills mounting up…" Hester sank down into a kitchen chair and put her head in her hands.

"Aidan, I've run out of money. Worse than that, for the first time in my life I've run out of ideas."

There were tears in Hester's eyes as she turned to face her stable manager. "It's over. I have no choice… I have to sell Blackthorn Farm."

CHAPTER 2

Sell Blackthorn Farm? Issie couldn't believe it. The farm was her favourite place in the whole world, and she knew how much her aunt loved it too.

She still remembered when Hester first bought the farm, complete with a decaying mansion, high in the hills outside Gisborne. Issie's mum had pronounced her sister "officially totally bonkers".

Mrs Brown worked for a law firm and was very practical about boring things like having a proper job. So when Hester broke the news that she was giving up her acting career, buying a rundown farm manor and becoming an animal trainer, Mrs Brown was far from impressed.

The whole farm, especially the manor, needed loads of work to restore it to its former glory. Loads of cash too.

Mrs Brown called Blackthorn Farm "Hester's Money Pit". Issie's aunt spent all of her savings restoring the buildings inside and out, including the stable block for her stunt horses.

Eventually, though, even Mrs Brown had to admit that Hester's hard work and determination had paid off. Hester's mad menagerie of movie-star animals – pigs, chickens, ducks, goats and especially horses – were considered to be the best in the business. Her Daredevil Ponies had worked on loads of films doing all sorts of stunts.

"It was all going so well!" Issie said. "I can't understand it. What happened?"

Mrs Brown sighed. "The movie business is unpredictable. Aidan told me they've been out of work ever since *The Palomino Princess*. There was a new project due to start filming this week and it fell through. Now Hester's been left with mountains of debt and no way to make any money!"

"But she can't sell the farm!" Issie said. "What about the horses?" Hester had over a dozen stunt horses in the stables at Blackthorn Farm.

There was silence on the phone. And then Mrs Brown finally spoke. "Aidan didn't say, but I guess they'll have to be sold as well."

"Mum! This is awful…" Issie felt close to tears.

"I know," Mrs Brown said gently. "Aidan is calling back soon. He says he has an idea that he wants to talk to you about, something that might help."

"I'm coming home now!" Issie hung up the phone. She turned around and saw Avery standing in the hallway behind her.

"I'm guessing she doesn't just want you to tidy your room then?" he said.

When Issie told Avery the bad news he immediately offered to give her a lift home. Issie gratefully accepted, putting her bike in the back of the Range Rover and clambering into the passenger seat. She spent the ride home in total silence, feeling sick with worry. Aunty Hess couldn't sell Blackthorn Farm. Things sounded pretty bad, but maybe there was still hope. What was this idea that Aidan wanted to talk to her about?

Issie didn't have long to wait before she found out. The phone was ringing as she ran in through the front door.

"I've got it!" she called, making a mad dash down the hallway to grab the receiver. She was still puffing and trying to catch her breath when she heard Aidan's voice at the other end of the line.

"Issie? Is that you?" She knew that they were in

the middle of a crisis here, but still Issie couldn't help smiling when she heard Aidan's voice. She hadn't seen him in ages and she had missed him. She pictured his face, the thick mop of black hair and the long fringe that hung down, almost hiding those startling blue eyes.

"Issie? Are you there?"

"Sorry, I'm still puffed from running to the phone," Issie panted.

"That's OK," Aidan said. "You don't need to talk anyway. Just listen. I have a plan to save the farm and I want you to hear it because I'm going to need your help." He paused. "Issie, I want to start a riding school."

"What?"

"My mum used to run one years ago when I was little," Aidan continued, "and I always thought Blackthorn Farm would be the perfect place to have one."

"But it's miles from anywhere!" Issie protested.

"I know," Aidan said, "but school holidays are about to start, right? We could run a school holiday camp with ponies. Kids could come and stay during the week and go home on the weekends and we could give them lessons."

"We?"

"That's where you come in," Aidan said. "I need

instructors. Hester and I have too much farmwork to do it all ourselves."

"But I'm not an instructor!" Issie squeaked.

"You've got your B certificate, haven't you? And don't Stella and Kate have theirs too? That means you can be junior instructors. Hester can run the school and you'll be her assistants."

"Does Hester think it's a good idea then?" Issie said.

"She will do once I tell her about it," Aidan said. Issie laughed, but he sounded serious. "You've got to help me do this, Issie. It's our last chance. I don't want Hester to lose the farm."

Issie took a deep breath. "When can you come and pick us up?" she said.

Issie needed to talk to Stella and Kate urgently – and she knew exactly where they would be, since today was rally day. She would find them at the pony club.

Some things never changed at Chevalier Point Pony Club. Take Natasha Tucker for instance. You would have thought, after all Issie and Natasha had been through together as stunt riders on the set of *The Palomino Princess*, that Natasha would have finally wanted to be friends. But no. From the moment the girls had arrived back at pony club this season, Natasha had become her same old super-snobby self. In fact, she was worse than ever. Issie had been really upset at first when Natasha had stopped speaking to her. Now she just tried to avoid her – which wasn't always easy.

"They must be here somewhere," Issie said, staring out of the window as her mum manoeuvred her car through the pony-club gates and into the parking area. Issie was so busy looking for her two best friends that she hardly noticed where her mum was driving until it was too late.

"No, Mum! Not here!" Issie shrieked as Mrs Brown pulled to a stop right next to the Tuckers' flashy blue and silver horse truck.

"What's wrong?"

"That's Natasha's truck!" groaned Issie.

"I thought you and Natasha were friends now?" Mrs Brown said.

"So did I," Issie sighed, "but it turns out that Natasha doesn't think so." Issie didn't know why Stuck-up Tucker was so against her, although Stella insisted that it was because Natasha was jealous.

"Jealous?" Issie didn't understand. "Jealous of what?"

"You and Dan!" Stella said. "She has got, like, a huge crush on him and you're always hanging out with him, which makes her blood boil."

It was true. Issie and Dan were pretty tight – but big deal! Stella and Kate and Ben were her friends too! Dan was most definitely not her boyfriend. Still, if Natasha wanted to be jealous of Issie's non-boyfriend then she guessed there wasn't much she could do about it – except stay out of Natasha's way.

"Mum? Do we have to park here? Can't we move?" Issie pleaded again. But it was too late because at that moment, a blonde girl with hair braided into ramrod-straight plaits emerged from behind the corner of the blue and silver horse truck. She was leading an elegant rose-grey gelding.

Issie attempted a cheery greeting. "Hi, Natasha!"

Natasha didn't smile back. "What are you doing here?" she said flatly. "It's a rally day and you don't have a horse to ride, do you?"

"Ummm... I'm looking for Stella and Kate," Issie faltered. "Have you seen them?"

"Why?" said Natasha. "What do you want them for?" Natasha's frosty stare made Issie start to babble and before she knew it she was telling Natasha all about Aidan's phone call.

As soon as she started, though, she wished she had kept her mouth shut. Natasha's face was like thunder. Even though she would never admit it, it was obvious that in some weird way Natasha was upset that Issie wasn't asking her to join them this time. Issie sighed. If she had actually asked her, Natasha would certainly have said no. Now, because she hadn't asked her, Natasha was in a total huff. You just couldn't win.

"So Aidan is looking for some pony-mad slaves to rope in to do all your aunt's donkey work yet again," Natasha harrumphed. "I hope you're not thinking of asking me this time because I've already done dung duty for her once and I'm not planning on falling for that again."

"It's not like you were her slave! Aunty Hess paid us to work on *The Palomino Princess*!" Issie said indignantly.

"What-ever!" said Natasha. "Anyway, I'd rather be riding my own horse than trying to teach some snot-nosed brats how to keep their hands steady. You probably won't even get a chance to ride. You'll be too busy mucking out the stalls and grooming all their ponies for them."

Natasha smirked at this put-down, then made a vague gesture across the club grounds to the far paddock. "Anyway, if you're looking for Stella and Kate, I think I saw them over by the main arena." And with that, she turned her back on Issie and began to busy herself with attaching Fabergé's bell boots.

Issie didn't care what Stuck-up Tucker said. Maybe the riding school would be a lot of hard work and not much actual riding. But it would still be fun just being near the horses, helping to groom them and look after them. She just hoped that Stella and Kate would both feel the same way. Aidan needed all three of them.

Issie found Stella and Kate with their horses, under the shade of the plane trees by the main arena. The girls had finished riding for the morning and were watching the other riders in the showjumping arena.

Stella was lying on the grass next to Coco, her little chocolate brown mare. She had taken off her riding helmet and her wild red curls were sticking out at funny angles with a flat patch on the top of her head where the helmet had been. Kate was standing next to her holding the reins of her rangy bay Thoroughbred, Toby. She was taller than the other two girls, even though they were all in the same form at Chevalier Point High School. Kate still had her helmet on and she wore her blonde bobbed hair tucked up neatly out of the way in a hairnet – which was actually a rule for club days although Stella clearly hadn't bothered. Stella wasn't very big on rules. Issie noticed that she wasn't even wearing her club tie underneath her navy vest.

"Issie! Ohmygod. What are you doing here?" Stella shrieked when she saw her best friend. She shrieked even louder when Issie told her about Aunt Hester's riding school.

"Us?" Stella shrieked. "Riding instructors!"

"Uh-huh," Issie said. "The kids are novices so we'll just be teaching them the basics. Plus, we'll have to help Hester to run the camp, doing all the other stuff like cooking meals and grooming the horses. She can't afford to pay us, but we get room and board. Plus you get to bring Toby and Coco with you and we can hack out across the farm after we finish schooling each day."

Stella grinned. "Cool. If I can bring Coco then I'm totally there!"

Issie knew it would be easy to convince Stella – she was mad keen on anything horsey. But sensible, practical Kate was a different story.

"Why is Hester running a riding school? I thought she trained movie horses," Kate said.

"Ummm… the movie business is having a few hiccups," Issie said. "Anyway, it's not just a riding school, it's like a camp for horsey kids like us. The riders come and stay at Blackthorn Farm for three weeks over the school holidays and learn to ride…" She saw Kate's hesitant expression. "Come on! It will be really good fun…"

"When do we go?"

"We need to spend the week before the kids arrive getting the camp ready. Aidan is coming with the horse truck to pick us up on Tuesday."

"That's only two days!" Kate boggled. "Issie, I don't know if I can. Mum will flip out if I tell her I'm going away for a whole month!"

"Please, Kate!" Issie begged. "I know it's short notice, but Aunty Hess needs us straightaway."

Issie had been desperately worried that Kate would say no. Of course she would be put off by the idea of suddenly changing her holiday plans and going all the way to Gisborne for a month. The problem was, she couldn't imagine going without Kate. Cool, calm Kate was a really good riding instructor; she was brilliant with kids and had loads of patience. All the junior riders at Chevalier Point totally adored her and Kate was always

Avery's first choice to fill in and teach the younger kids if an instructor failed to turn up for a practice session.

Kate looked thoughtful. "Issie, do you think you could get your mum to ask my mum? If your mum has OKed it, she'd have to say yes. Besides, I've stayed at Hester's before and she let me go that time, didn't she...?" Kate was smiling now. "And if I can take Toby with me, how excellent would that be?"

Issie squealed and threw her arms around Kate. "I knew you'd say yes! Oh, this is going to be so cool!"

The only thing left to organise now was Storm. Issie would miss him so much, but she was sure that Avery would take good care of the colt and Blaze while she was away. Avery had looked after Blaze when she was in foal and Issie was away working on *The Palomino Princess*. She knew that Avery would be more than happy to take care of Storm and Blaze while she was gone. She saw him over by the clubhouse and set off to ask him.

"I can't," Avery told her. Issie couldn't believe it.

"Issie, you know that normally I would do it," Avery continued. "The problem is, I was planning to go to

Gisborne myself in a week. It's the Horse of the Year Show. I'm taking Dan and Ben down to prepare their horses to compete in the showjumping. This is the first time Dan will have a chance to compete on his new horse. We've been planning it for ages."

Of course! How could Issie have forgotten? The Horse of the Year was the biggest event on the equestrian calendar.

Avery looked concerned. "I'm sorry, Issie. I can look after Storm and Blaze for the first week, but then we're trucking Madonna and Max to Gisborne to start training there and I'm afraid that leaves you stuck – unless you figure out a solution."

Issie was devastated. This completely ruined their plans. She couldn't leave Storm behind with no one to check on him and care for him each day. And she couldn't take the colt with her. There was no way he was old enough to travel all the way to Blackthorn Farm. The trip to Gisborne took most of the day in the horse truck, much too far for a three-month-old colt. There was only one solution, Issie decided. She couldn't go.

"Don't be ridiculous!" Mrs Brown said when Issie met her back at the car and broke the bad news. "Of course you're going. It's all arranged."

"But, Mum, I can't leave Storm and Blaze alone."

"I'll look after them," Mrs Brown said confidently.

"You? But, Mum, you don't even like horses…"

"Oh, for goodness sake, Isadora," Mrs Brown said. "OK, I think we're all aware that I'm not exactly Pippa Funnell, but it's not like you're asking me to ride at Badminton, is it? I've been around them for long enough now and I think it's perfectly within my capabilities to go and check on your ponies each day. I'll make sure they've got food and water and that Storm hasn't got himself tangled in the electric fence!"

"Really?"

"Absolutely," Mrs Brown smiled. "They will be just fine, I promise you."

Aunt Hester was thrilled that evening when Issie phoned her with the good news. "Aidan's quite convinced that this riding-school plan will save our bacon – and I certainly hope he's right," Hester said. "Is your mum OK about you coming here for the holidays? I haven't ruined any family plans, have I?"

"Mum's been great!" Issie said. "And she talked to Mrs Knight and convinced her to let Kate come. She's even looking after Blaze and Storm while I'm away."

"Well, well," Hester said. "It might not be too late for that sister of mine to turn horsey after all."

"I know!" Issie said. "I can't believe it's all organised and we're really coming. By this time tomorrow we'll be at Blackthorn Farm."

CHAPTER 3

"We're nearly there!" Issie pressed her face up against the window at the back of the truck cab and mouthed the words through the glass at Stella and Kate.

"What's she saying?" Kate was frustrated. "I can't hear her through the glass!"

"Issie!" Stella shouted back. "We can't hear you! What are you saying?"

The cab of Aunt Hester's horse truck wasn't big enough for all the girls to fit up front so it had been decided that Issie would travel in the cab with Aidan while Kate and Stella rode in the back.

The girls didn't mind riding in the back. The truck was fitted out a bit like a camper van, with a shower, kitchenette and bunk beds, and it was comfy enough travelling on the bench seats. Plus, from where they sat, Stella and Kate could keep an eye on Toby and Coco who were travelling at the very back of the truck in their stalls. The girls could see Issie and Aidan too by peering through the little window with very thick glass at the back of the truck cab.

Issie tapped on the glass and tried again. "I said… We're nearly there!"

"Oh, give up, Issie!" Aidan grinned. "They'll figure it out for themselves soon enough. We're about to reach the turn-off."

The six-hour drive to Blackthorn Farm had somehow seemed shorter this time. That might have been because she and Aidan hadn't stopped talking from the moment Issie got into the truck. There was so much for them to catch up on.

"I haven't seen Nightstorm since he was two days old," Aidan said, "so that would make him…"

"Three months old!" Issie said. "He's already almost thirteen hands. Avery reckons he'll grow to sixteen-two, and he's so beautiful. He's losing all his foal fluff and he's got the most amazing deep bay coat, with a thick black mane and tail and black points. He looks so cute with his white blaze. He's exactly like his mum in some ways, but

34

he's kind of like Marius too. He has his own personality though – he's really smart. I taught him to wear a halter in just one day."

Aidan pushed his long, dark fringe out of his eyes and looked at Issie. "It must have been hard to leave him."

"Uh-huh," Issie said. She didn't want to tell Aidan that she had been in floods of tears when she said goodbye to the colt last night. She knew it was only a month, but it seemed like such a long time to be away from him when he was so young.

"Well, I'm really glad you came," Aidan said softly. Then he realised he sounded mushy and tried to make up for it by adding, "Ummm… cos Hester really needs your help."

Issie smiled. "Hester says you've been schooling up a few of the Blackthorn Ponies that we caught when we were here last time."

The Blackthorn Ponies were a wild herd that roamed the hills around Blackthorn Farm. On her last holiday at the farm Issie and Aidan had saved the herd from a cull. Most of the ponies had been sent to new homes, but Hester had kept a few of them with her at the farm.

"That's part of the problem," Aidan continued. "The cost of those extra ponies adds up fast. Hester has thirteen horses now – that's a lot of farrier bills and hard feed."

"So the riding school will cover the bills?"

"Uh-huh," Aidan said. "We won't make a fortune out of it, but hopefully we'll make enough to keep the farm going until the next movie job comes along."

Issie looked worried. "And what if another film job doesn't come along?"

"Something will turn up soon," Aidan said reassuringly. "I'm sure everything will be fine."

"But, Aidan, what if it's not fine?"

"Well, if things got really tight, I guess we'd have to sell some of the horses," said Aidan quietly. "Diablo and Stardust are experienced stunt horses – they're both worth quite a lot. But if that's not enough…"

"Then what?"

"Then Hester will have to sell Blackthorn Farm."

For the first time since they had set off on this trip, silence settled over the truck cab. Issie stared out of the windows at the road ahead and couldn't help wondering if this would be the last time she would be making this journey.

By the time the horse truck came through the narrow Gisborne gorge and began to travel up through the green cornfields towards the high country, Issie had pulled herself together again. In fact, she was positively filled with resolve.

"You're right. Things will be fine!" she said firmly, smiling at Aidan. The riding school would make enough money – or they'd think of something else. No matter what, there was no way her aunt was going to lose Blackthorn Farm.

Half an hour later, they reached the crest of a very steep hill. To the right, Issie could see the bright blue sea of the Gisborne coastline, and on the left was farmland and forest. Up ahead she could see a gravel road that veered to the left off the main highway.

"We're here!"

Aidan turned off down the private road, slowing down a gear as the truck struck gravel. Issie watched as the trees closed in around her and the truck became cocooned in the dense native forest that bordered the sides of the driveway that led to Blackthorn Farm. Low-hanging pohutukawa branches scraped against the roof of the truck.

"I keep telling Hester we need to prune the trees back to get the truck through," Aidan said as he heard the branches scraping the roof above him. "She just tells me to 'add it to the endless list of things that need doing'!"

A few more scrapes and bangs later and they had emerged into the bright sunlight once more. Issie's heart leapt when she saw the familiar sight of the cherry trees, their white and pink petals falling in a snowy carpet on the circular lawn in front of Blackthorn Manor.

The tumbledown mansion was just as she remembered. The enormous two-storeyed country manor must once have been very grand, but was, she noted with fresh eyes, definitely rickety and in desperate need of a new coat of white paint.

"It must have been horrible being here over the past couple of months. You know, with all those movies cancelling at the last minute."

"Actually," Aidan said, "this will sound weird, but it's been great. I mean, yeah, it's been stressful, especially for Hester. But having no film work has meant that I could spend more time riding. I've been doing loads of training sessions on Destiny."

"Like movie training?" Issie asked.

Aidan shook his head. "Showjumping. Destiny's a natural jumper. He picks his feet up really cleanly and never knocks the rails."

"How high have you been jumping?"

"He can do about a metre twenty," Aidan said. "Easily big enough to put him in the prize money."

"What prize money?" Issie was confused.

"The Horse of the Year Show," Aidan said. "I haven't asked Hester yet, but I was thinking of entering him in the novice horse class."

"Do you think he can win?"

Aidan nodded. "Yep – and it's decent prize money too. The Horse of the Year is the richest competition in the whole Southern hemisphere. There's half a million dollars in prize money. If Destiny and I win the novice class, that's worth $10,000."

"$10,000?"

"There'll be loads of competition though," Aidan continued. "There are riders from all over the country coming down for it."

"I know," Issie said. "Tom is coming down next week. He's bringing Dan and Ben. I think Dan's riding in the novice class too."

Aidan seemed to go very quiet at this news. When he finally spoke his voice sounded quite different. "That guy Dan. You go to pony club with him, right?"

"Uh-huh," said Issie.

"And he's, like, a friend of yours?" Issie nodded. Aidan went quiet again for a moment.

"Is he your boyfriend?"

Issie was stunned. She hadn't been expecting this. "No," she said, "no, he's not." Aidan looked relieved.

"Hester is probably waiting for us down at the stables," he said. "We'll drive straight through to unload the horses." He nosed the truck to the right of the circular lawn so that they swept right past the front door of the manor and headed down the limestone drive towards the stables.

"Issie?"

"Uh-huh."

"You know what I said before? About me being glad that you were here? Well, I am, Issie. I'm really glad. It seems like ages since I saw you and…" Aidan stopped paying attention to the road and stared at Issie. He was fidgeting nervously with the sleeve of his tartan shirt. "The thing is, I've been wanting to ask you something the whole way down here…"

He was suddenly interrupted by Issie who let out a loud shriek. "Stop the truck, Aidan! You're going to hit him!"

Aidan's foot instinctively went for the brake as he turned to see what had made Issie shout out. In front of them, galloping straight for their truck, was a pony.

"Aidan!" Issie yelled again.

"I see him!" said Aidan, sounding the horn at the pony.

"What's wrong with him?" Issie asked. "Why doesn't he get out of the way?" The pony was still galloping towards them. There was no way the truck could stop in time. They would hit him for sure.

"You've got to stop!" Issie shouted.

"I'm trying!" said Aidan. "It's not that simple – we have horses in the truck to think about!"

Issie realised that he was right. If Aidan slammed the brakes on too quickly then Toby and Coco would be thrown forward violently and might be badly hurt. But if Aidan didn't brake fast enough then the poor pony that was bearing down on them would be killed.

It felt as if everything was in slow motion as the pony continued to gallop at them and tyres skidded against the limestone gravel as Aidan tried to stop. The horrible squeal of truck brakes filled Issie's ears, overwhelming her in a rush of memory. She had a sickening sense of déjà vu – as if she was reliving that awful day at Chevalier Point. The day when Mystic had been killed. It was nearly two years ago now that the accident had happened. Her mind always got so confused when she tried to think about that day.

Issie remembered trying to stop the runaway horses from heading out on to the main road, her sense of horror as Mystic had reared up to face the truck. Then she was falling backwards and the tarmac was rushing up to meet her. There had been a sickening crack as her helmet hit the road, and the taste of blood in her mouth before it all went black. After that, she couldn't recall anything until she woke up hours later in the hospital with her mother calling her name. Her mother told her what had happened. She explained how Mystic had saved Issie by throwing her clear of the truck. Issie still remembered the desperate expression on her mother's face as she struggled to answer her question. "Mum? What about Mystic? Is Mystic OK?"

It was the very worst moment in Issie's life. Her first pony Mystic had been her best friend. She had loved him so completely, so deeply. Losing him was like losing her own soul.

Now, suddenly, she was living through it all over again. Only this time she was watching it all from inside the truck, powerless to do anything as she sat waiting for the awful, inevitable moment of collision with the horse in front of her.

Issie shut her eyes and held her breath. She couldn't bear to look. Instinctively she put her arms on the dashboard to brace herself for the impact. A few seconds later, when the crash didn't come, she opened her eyes again.

The truck had stopped. The horse was nowhere to be seen and Issie suddenly realised that she was crying and shaking and Aidan was holding her tight in his arms. "It's OK," he was saying, "it's all right. We didn't hit him."

"Aidan!" Issie felt like she couldn't breathe. "We were going to hit him. I was sure we were going to…"

"Shhhh, it's OK. I know. I thought we were going to hit him too. He got out of the way just in time. Are you OK?" Aidan let go of Issie and sat back in his seat.

"Uh-huh." Issie dried her eyes. "I'm fine."

"That was close, huh?"

"Where did that horse come from?" Issie wondered. "He seemed to come out of nowhere."

"He must have jumped out of his paddock again." Aidan shook his head. "That's the third time this week. He might have escaped the truck, but I'm pretty sure that this time Hester is going to kill him!"

"You mean he's done this before?"

"Yeah. Last time he jumped out, he managed to get into the garden shed and ate all of the dog biscuits. He is totally crazy, that pony. Hester is so fed up with him. She can't afford to put up deer fences to keep him in – and, knowing Comet, he'd probably jump over them anyway!"

"Comet?" Issie said.

"Uh-huh," Aidan replied. "He's one of the Blackthorn Ponies that Hester decided to keep. Although I think she's been regretting the decision ever since."

Just as he said this, Issie saw her aunt emerge from the rear of Blackthorn Manor. She had a makeshift lead rope in her hands that she had made out of the belt from her dress. She was using it to lead a cheeky-looking skewbald. The pony, for he was just a pony and couldn't have been more than fourteen-two hands, was skipping merrily at her side. He didn't seem to notice or care that Hester was looking at him with a murderous expression. The skewbald looked so pleased with himself that, despite the heart attack he had just given her, Issie couldn't help but immediately have a soft spot for him.

"So that's Comet?"

"The one and only," Aidan said darkly. "The skewbald that no paddock can hold."

As Comet came closer, Issie could see that he was actually rather pretty. The pony was a chestnut with white patches, and he had white socks and a broad, white stripe down his nose. Comet was sturdy and muscular, like all wild Gisborne hill ponies. He had solid legs with thick cannon bones, strong shoulders and powerful hindquarters made for jumping – a fact which he was clearly using to his advantage to get out of the paddock whenever he liked. The pony's conformation was powerful, but it was his eyes that had Issie totally bewitched. Those eyes! They burnt with an intensity that she hadn't seen before in any horse.

Comet seemed thrilled that everyone was paying him so much attention. As he danced along at Hester's side, Issie could have sworn he had the attitude of a champion racehorse. In his mind, this pony wasn't little at all. He was a colossus.

"Comet! Stand still, naughty pony!" Hester growled. Then she turned to Issie and Aidan. "Isadora! Lovely to see you. I take it you've already met Comet?"

"You could say that," Issie smiled.

"Well, my favourite niece, as you can see, this place hasn't changed a bit – it's still completely mad!" Hester said. "Welcome back to Blackthorn Farm."

CHAPTER 4

"You mean we were nearly hit by a comet?" Stella said. She and Kate had emerged from the truck and were totally confused by what had just happened.

"No," Issie giggled. "We nearly hit him. Comet is a horse!" She gestured towards the skewbald pony who was still skipping about as Aunt Hester tried to hold him with the belt off her dress.

"He escaped on to the driveway and we nearly ran him over," Aidan explained.

"Are Toby and Coco OK?" Hester asked.

"They're both fine," Stella said. "They scrambled a bit when the truck stopped suddenly, but they didn't fall over or anything."

"Let's get them unloaded," Kate suggested. "We can

check them over properly in the loose box once we take off their floating bandages."

Since the truck had been forced to stop halfway down the driveway it seemed easier to simply unload the horses there and walk them the rest of the way.

Toby and Coco came down the ramp with their ears pricked and their heads held high, as horses do whenever they arrive somewhere new. When he saw them Comet gave a whinny of greeting. His whole body reverberated as his clarion call rang out, shaking with a neigh of excitement at having new horses for company.

Hester glared at him. "Oh, do behave yourself, Comet! You really are the most troublesome pony." She turned to the girls. "I don't want you to think they're all this bad. Most of the Blackthorn Ponies we have here are very well schooled. I've got several new horses that are perfect learners' ponies, ideal for the riding school. Come on, let's put your horses away and then you can meet some of them."

The stable block at Blackthorn Farm was built from the same white-painted weatherboards as the manor. Inside it was like a giant barn, with bales of hay stacked up in one corner, a storage room for tack and two rows of loose boxes. On the door of each loose box a horse's head was carved into the honey-coloured wood above a plaque with the horse's name inscribed on it.

Issie pushed open the vast wooden sliding door and walked inside, followed by Stella and Kate leading Coco and Toby, and Aunt Hester, still with her makeshift dress-belt halter, hanging on to Comet.

"You can put your horses in the first two boxes on the left there, girls," Hester said.

"What about Comet?" asked Issie.

"I don't usually box him," Hester said. "Blackthorn Ponies don't really like it in the stable as a rule. They prefer to graze out. But I might have to make an exception in Comet's case – at least if he's in a loose box he won't be able to jump out!"

Hester popped Comet in the box next to Coco's. The stall was freshly mucked out with clean straw on the floor and water in the trough. Comet gave his new home a rather bored once-over and then craned his neck desperately over the Dutch door, whinnying to get attention. Coco stuck her head out of her stall and returned his call.

"Shhh! Coco!" Stella said, giggling. "He's a naughty pony. Don't encourage him!"

As they walked down the rows of loose boxes the girls could see familiar faces poking out of the top of each stall door. First in the row were the three palominos, Paris, Nicole and Stardust, the mares they had ridden when they were working as stunt riders on *The Palomino Princess*. Issie stopped and fed a carrot to Stardust, running a hand through her silver-white mane, admiring the rich treacle sheen of her coat. "Remember me, girl?" she asked softly.

Her question was answered by a nicker from the stall next door as a black and white face emerged. "Diablo!" Issie grinned at him. Diablo was Aunt Hester's favourite stunt horse, a piebald Quarter Horse that could do all sorts of tricks, including playing dead when a gun was fired – a trick that had almost scared Issie and her friends out of their wits the last time they were at Blackthorn Farm.

In the stall next to Diablo was the enormous draught horse Dolomite. The big bay with the white blaze stood at nearly sixteen-three hands, while, in the stall right next to him, was Titan, the dinky miniature pony who couldn't have been more than ten hands high!

"Dolly and Titan obviously aren't any use as riding-school ponies," Hester said. "You'd need a ladder to mount Dolly."

"What about Titan?" Stella asked. "Couldn't one of the little kids ride on him?"

Hester shook her head. "Titan is a true miniature, a Falabella. They're not really bred as riding ponies; they can only handle very light weights on their back – although he can tow a cart."

In the stall next to Titan was a dark brown pony who was around thirteen hands high. "This is Molly, one of my new ones," Hester said. "She's a Blackthorn Pony that I've been schooling up. Very well mannered – the perfect learner's pony."

"How many ponies will you need?" asked Issie.

"That depends on how many students enroll," Hester said. "The ad has only been up on the *PONY Magazine* website for a few days and we already have five keen pupils lined up."

"Do any of them actually know anything about riding?" Kate asked Hester.

"The twins, Tina and Trisha, have experience," said Hester. "They're ten years old and they've been having weekly lessons since they turned eight apparently. I was planning to put them on Paris and Nicole. They'll be perfect for more advanced riders. The youngest rider so far is Kitty – she's eight and mad keen on ponies according to her mum, although her brother George, who is ten, sounds like a handful. Both of them have had riding lessons, so they know the basics."

"Which ponies will you put Kitty and George on?" asked Issie.

"I'm not sure about George, but I was thinking that Kitty could ride Timmy, the sweet chestnut with the star on his forehead. He's a Blackthorn Pony too, no vices and thoroughly bombproof," Hester said. "The oldest girl is eleven. Her name is Kelly-Anne and she insists she's a bit of an expert – but she seems utterly green to me, if you know what I mean. I'm going to put her on Julian. He's a bit of a plodder, quite safe for an absolute beginner."

Issie and Stella exchanged nervous glances. Up until now the idea of running a riding school had seemed like fun. But now that they were here it all seemed kind of daunting. Next Monday they would have actual pupils arriving. And some of the riders weren't much younger than they were. What would they say when they saw that their instructors were just a bunch of kids?

"I thought you three could draw up a lesson plan and a timetable this afternoon, then we've got time to iron out the kinks during the week before the riders arrive," Hester continued.

"Lesson plan?" Stella squeaked. "Won't you be doing that? I mean, we won't actually be taking the lessons all by ourselves, will we?"

Hester shook her head. "I'm not expecting you to do everything by yourselves. But it's good to have a game plan so you can cope without me. Aidan and I have a lot of work to do just keeping the farm running so it's possible you'll be left alone in charge at least some of the time." Hester noticed the terrified looks on the three girls' faces. "Something wrong?"

"Ummm… no…" Issie managed.

"Good!" Hester said brightly. "Well, I think that's enough of a tour of the stables for today. You can meet the rest of the ponies later. Shall we get back up to the house and you can unpack your things? You've all got your usual rooms. I hope that's OK?"

Issie's bedroom was the first room off the landing at the top of the grand wooden staircase. She threw her bags down on the enormous four-poster bed and then threw herself down next to them. The huge room was papered

52

with antique horsey wallpaper and hanging above the fireplace was an enormous oil painting of Avignon, Aunt Hester's great grey Warmblood stallion. In the portrait Avignon was running free, his beautiful silver mane flowing in the wind. Issie lay on the bed and gazed up at the painting, taking in the beauty of the horse, the arch of his neck, the flare of his nostrils, the deep, dark eyes staring back at her.

"All settled in?" Aidan's voice startled her. He was standing in the doorway holding a duffel bag. "I'm moving into the last room down the end of the hall."

Issie was confused. "Why aren't you in your cottage down by the stables?"

"It made sense to move out," Aidan said matter-of-factly. "We needed somewhere to put all the kids so we turned the cottage into a sort of dormitory. I'm staying here in the main house until they leave." He stepped into Issie's room and shut the door conspiratorially behind him. "Hey," he said in a low, stagey whisper, "we need to have a secret meeting."

"What about?"

"Dinner," he said. "I want to sort out a roster before the kids get here. We need to stop Hester spending too much time in the kitchen – for obvious reasons!"

Aidan was right. Issie's aunt might be able to run a riding school. But it was an entirely different matter to feed a riding school. Hester was, quite possibly, the world's worst cook. Her dinners usually ended up as blackened, inedible mounds in the oven. Her baking was so bad that even Butch, the resident farm pig, turned his nose up at it. Unfortunately Hester had already been in the kitchen that very morning. When the girls came downstairs after unpacking they found her waiting for them with a plate of scones for afternoon tea. They were like bricks with raisins in them.

Stella picked one up and took a bite. She instantly regretted it. "Ow, I fink oif broken a twooth!"

"There is no way she's cooking dinner," Issie muttered to Aidan as she choked down a mouthful of her scone.

"We'll sort out that roster," Aidan agreed.

Cooking and cleaning rosters, riding timetables, lesson plans. There was lots to be prepared before the new pupils arrived. "Can't we do it all later?" Stella grumbled as they sat down at the kitchen table with pens and sheets of paper. "I mean, it's only Tuesday. We have nearly a week to get all this done and it's a lovely sunny afternoon and we've been cooped up in the truck all day. I want to go riding."

"We didn't come here for a holiday!" Kate said. "We've got work to do. Don't you want to be organised when the riders arrive on Monday?"

Hester surprised everyone by agreeing with Stella. "We could work on the rosters and timetables tonight," she suggested, "and I've got a stable full of riding-school ponies who could all do with some exercise." She looked at her watch. "If we get down there now, there's enough time for a quick bit of schooling in the arena before dinner."

Nobody needed convincing. The girls dashed up to their rooms to get their jodhpurs on while Aidan and Hester went ahead to the stables to get the ponies ready.

"I saw the cutest little grey pony grazing next to the arena when we arrived. I wonder if I can try that one?" Stella said.

"I like the chestnut one with the star on his forehead and the three white socks," Kate said. "What's his name again?"

"His name is Timmy. And your ankles will drag on the ground if you ride him!" Issie giggled. "Hester will probably put you on one of the palominos."

Issie knew which horse she would be getting. Hester was bound to put her on Stardust, after they had bonded so well on the set of *The Palomino Princess*.

As they neared the stables it looked like Issie was right. When Aidan emerged from the stalls he had Stardust all saddled up and her reins in his right hand. It seemed like a lifetime since Issie had ridden the pretty palomino. She felt a shiver of anticipation as she strode towards the mare. "Hey, girl." Issie reached out a hand to stroke her glossy, treacle-coloured neck. She was about to take the reins from Aidan when she heard her Aunt Hester's voice behind her.

"Issie! There you are! Come with me. I've got your horse ready too."

Issie was confused. "But I thought I'd be riding Stardust, Aunty Hess?"

"Oh, I'm sorry, dear. I thought I told you," Hester said. "Aidan is on Stardust today. I was hoping you would take on a new mount that really needs the work."

"What?"

"The skewbald troublemaker," Hester said, gesturing to the last stall in the loose-box row. "I want you to ride Comet."

As if on cue at the mention of his name, Comet thrust his chestnut and white face over the Dutch door and let out a cheeky whinny. Issie looked suspiciously at the skewbald pony.

"He needs riding. He gets so frightfully bored standing in the loose box," Hester said. "It's his own fault of course. If he wasn't such a troublemaker, I'd let him back out to graze with the others... I mean, you can't leave him in the paddock because he jumps out and you can't leave him in the loose box because he tries to destroy it."

As if to confirm this, Comet began banging and scraping the bottom half of the Dutch door with his hoof. *Get me out of here!* he seemed to be saying.

"Naughty Comet! Stop that!" Issie said firmly. She grabbed the skewbald by the reins, unbolted the stall door and led him out into the yard.

Hester had already tacked him up for her and Issie noticed that Comet looked quite different in a saddle and bridle. He was one of those skewbalds with vigorous splashes of white all over his withers and rump. They trickled down his legs finishing up with four white socks – a bit like someone had spilt a can of white paint over him. Even his chestnut tail looked like it had been streaked with a paintbrush.

Once you put a saddle on, though, Comet's colouring was less obvious. The saddle blanket completely covered up the white marks on his withers and back. He almost looked like an ordinary chestnut with four white socks, except when you looked from the other side you could see a big splodge of white on his hindquarters that looked a bit like a map of India.

As Issie led Comet out into the yard and over to the mounting block the pony danced along beside her, lifting his legs up in a high-stepping trot. When he was sure that everyone was watching him he raised his head and gave a high-spirited nicker, calling out to the other ponies.

"Comet! Stop being such a show-off!" The skewbald skipped about on the spot as Issie tried to steady him long enough to put her foot in the stirrup.

Issie knew she needed to be firm with this pony. Comet was green and he had shocking bad manners. Ponies were supposed to walk quietly beside you, not skip about. But she didn't have the heart to be too tough on him. There was something about his grand attitude and silly antics that just made her want to giggle. Comet strutted about as if he was a superstar instead of just a little skewbald gelding in the paddock at Hester's house. Besides, Issie was beginning to realise that Comet didn't respond well to authority. He was a stroppy pony and if she wanted to bond with him, she was going to have to do things his way.

"Steady, Comet!" Issie gave up on using the mounting block as the pony kept dancing around her. As Comet circled she moved swiftly with him, slipping her foot into the stirrup and, before the pony even knew what was happening, she was bouncing up into the saddle and had landed lightly on his back. "Good boy!"

There is that moment when you sit on a horse for the very first time and you ask yourself, *How does it feel up here? Are we right for each other? Do we click?* You can never really know for sure straightaway. It takes a long time to get to know a horse. But in those first minutes in the saddle, as you ask them to walk, trot and canter for the first time, you get an inkling, almost like a sixth sense that tells you whether you really belong together.

Right now, Issie didn't realise it but she was unconsciously, instinctively, feeling this new horse out. She adjusted her position and felt the sturdiness of Comet's stocky frame, compact and solid underneath her. He was only fourteen-two, which meant that officially he qualified as a pony, not a hack, and yet Issie could sense that he had the attitude of a much larger horse.

As she gathered Comet up and asked him to step forward into a walk and then a trot, Issie felt almost instantly that he was exactly the sort of horse she liked – responsive and peppy. Issie only had to give him the lightest touch with her legs to get him moving.

"Take him on a lap or two around the arena to get used to his paces," Hester advised her. Issie nodded and asked Comet to trot. He did so immediately, his stride covering the ground in a floating trot with his hocks coming underneath him nicely. His canter too was bouncy and active. Issie felt a thrill of excitement tingle up her spine.

"He's got lovely paces, Aunty Hess!"

Hester smiled. "He's still green, but he has loads of potential. I think you'll get on famously."

As if to confirm this, Comet raised his head and let out another loud whinny, calling out to the other horses as if to say, "Look at me!" Issie laughed and gave Comet a slappy pat on his glossy neck.

"Well, Comet already thinks he's famous – I guess that's a good start."

CHAPTER 5

What is a riding instructor supposed to look like? Issie had fretted about it all morning as she got dressed. Today the riding-school kids would all be arriving and Issie, Stella and Kate had to look the part and impress their new pupils.

She thought about Tom Avery. He always cut such a commanding figure at the Chevalier Point Pony Club in his cream jodhpurs, tweed hacking jacket and a cheesecutter cap on top of his thick thatch of dark, curly hair. A riding crop was permanently in his hand – not to use on the horses, but to thwack against his long leather boots for emphasis when making a point. Issie had flirted with the idea of wearing a cheesecutter cap like Tom's when she was getting dressed, but decided that it looked a bit too much. She had decided to go with the riding crop, however, and she carried this in her right hand as she walked into the kitchen.

"Ohhh, I wish I'd thought of that," said Stella. Stella and Kate both had on their best instructor outfits too. Like Issie, they were wearing long boots and jods. Stella had on a pink Ralph Lauren polo shirt and Kate was wearing her short-sleeved shirt and her Chevalier Point Pony Club tie, which looked very smart.

"When are they due to arrive?" Kate asked, pacing back and forth, too nervous to eat her toast, which was going cold on the kitchen table.

"Any time now," said Issie. "Hester went off in the horse truck an hour ago to pick them up at the train station."

"Do we need to go down to the stables then?" asked Stella. "Hester said we should meet her there to welcome them."

"I guess so," Issie said, looking around nervously. "Hey, where's Aidan?"

"He's meeting us down there," Kate said. "He said he had to finish fixing something. I heard him hammering." It turned out that Aidan had been adding a new top railing to the paddock closest to the stables.

"I've made the fence half a metre higher all the way around," Aidan said with satisfaction as he threw his tool belt down in the corner of the stables.

"So you think it will hold him?" asked Issie.

Aidan nodded. "With that new rail the fence is almost one metre fifty. It would hold a deer. There's no way that little skewbald Houdini is escaping again."

"Poor Comet," Issie said. "He's been so fed up with being stabled all week. I bet he can't wait to get back outside."

Since their arrival at Blackthorn Farm, Issie had spent all her spare time riding Comet. Not that she had much spare time. Hester hadn't been kidding when she said there was a lot to get ready before the kids arrived. The ad on the *PONY Magazine* website had been successful. There were now eight riders signed up to arrive today at Blackthorn Farm Riding School.

"They should be here by now," Aidan said. "It only takes half an hour to drive back here from the train station…"

As he said this, there was a cacophony of barking as Hester's dogs, Nanook the Newfoundland, Strudel the golden retriever and Taxi the black and white sheepdog, all bounded out of the door of the stables to greet the horse truck that was pulling up in the driveway.

"That'll be them now," Aidan said.

"Well, shall we go and meet them then?" asked Issie, although she showed no signs of moving.

"Is my tie straight?" Kate asked nervously.

"I feel like I'm going to throw up," groaned Stella.

"There you are!" Hester said as the girls finally emerged through the wide sliding doors at the front of the stables. The young riders had all emerged from the truck with their bags and were standing beside Hester, staring back at the girls expectantly.

"Everyone, I'd like you to meet your instructors," Hester said. "This is Isadora, Stella and Kate. These girls are senior members of the Chevalier Point Pony Club. They are all B certificate riders with their own horses and loads of experience under their belts. They will be your tutors here at Blackthorn Farm Riding School and I want you to listen to them and do as they say at all times." The kids all nodded at this.

"You can leave your bags here for the moment," Hester said. "You'll be staying in the stable manager's cottage, but first I'm sure you want to meet the horses you'll be riding."

The riders all followed her through the stable doors and there were gasps of amazement from a couple of the younger ones as they saw just how vast and impressive the stables were once you got inside. Hester led them through to the centre of the stable block where a row of hay bales had been piled up to serve as seats.

"We've matched you up with your mounts based on your ages and riding abilities," Hester explained. "In the stalls here today are the horses that you'll be riding for the next three weeks."

Hester began with the two red-headed girls sitting on the hay bales at the end. The girls were so similar they were clearly identical twins. "This is Tina and her sister Trisha," Hester said. "They're from Wellington. How old are you, girls?"

"Ten," said Trisha.

"Tina and Trisha attend their local riding school each week. Is that right?" Tina and Trisha nodded vigorously. "You girls will be on Paris and Nicole," Hester told them. "Matching hair and matching horses!" Tina and Trisha looked pleased with this and instantly began discussing between themselves which one would have Paris and which one would get Nicole.

The next two girls were much younger, perhaps around eight. "Lucy and Sophie have only had a few riding lessons. They can do the basics like rising to trot,"

Hester explained to Issie, Stella and Kate. Then she turned to the two girls. "We've put you on Molly and Pippen. Lucy, you've got Pippen; he's the little grey in the stable here."

"He's beautiful!" Lucy said breathlessly. Sophie was just as impressed with Molly.

"These will be your ponies for the holidays. You'll be totally responsible for them and will feed, groom and care for them as well as riding them, OK?"

Lucy and Sophie were instantly up from the hay bales and glued to their ponies' sides. Sophie even produced a carrot that she had been carrying in her pocket for the whole trip to the farm in anticipation of this moment. She held out her palm to feed it to the eager Molly.

Hester moved on to a girl with white blonde hair and a boy standing next to her who had the same hair and was clearly her brother. "Kitty and George..." Hester continued, "who are both horse-mad according to their mum."

"I'm not horse-mad," George said. "Kitty is. Mum makes me have lessons and she made me come on this stupid holiday because she couldn't be bothered booking two school holiday programmes. I'd rather be riding a BMX."

Hester looked slightly taken aback at this. "Well, George, how about if you ride Diablo?" she said. "He's the perfect colour for a cowboy like you and he knows all the best tricks. He can count to ten with his hoof, you know." George looked quite impressed by this. Kitty, on the other hand, was standing there quietly, not daring to say a word. It was almost as if she couldn't believe her luck being here at all. Unlike her brother, she obviously adored horses. She looked so desperate to ride a horse, any horse, that you could tell it wouldn't matter which.

Kitty," Hester said, "I think we'll put you on Timmy." Hester opened the top door of a loose box to her right and there stood a chubby little chestnut pony with a star on his forehead and three white socks. He was quite clearly one of the Blackthorn Ponies, stocky with a shaggy mane and tail.

"I love chestnuts!" Kitty said. "They are my absolute favourite colour."

"Well, that's worked out perfectly then," said Hester.

She continued along the queue to the second boy who also looked about eight years old. He had a thick mop of dark brown hair and chubby cheeks. Hester looked at him suspiciously as if he might start on about BMX bikes too if she gave him the chance. "You'll be on Glennie,

Arthur." Hester gestured to the cattle pens just outside the back door where a dapple-grey Blackthorn Pony had his head over the fence and was watching them intently.

They had now reached the last child in the row, a sullen-looking girl with dark hair cut into a blunt-fringed bob. "And last but not least we have Kelly-Anne," Hester said. "Kelly-Anne will be on Julian."

Kelly-Anne looked at Julian as if he were something she'd had to scrape off the bottom of her riding boot. Julian, who was a rather ill-tempered little brown butterball of a pony, stared straight back at her with exactly the same expression.

"He looks useless!" Kelly-Anne said. "I don't want him. I want that one!" She pointed across the stable at Comet who was minding his own business for once and standing peacefully with his head over the loose-box door.

"Kelly-Anne, I'm sorry, but at this school you ride the horse you're given," Hester said quite patiently. "Comet is not a beginner's pony."

"I'm not a beginner. I'm a really good rider, so I want the best horse," Kelly-Anne piped up.

"Have you been riding long, dear?" Hester asked. "Do you go to pony club or do you have a local riding school?"

"No," Kelly-Anne said dismissively. "I don't like pony club, it's dumb. Besides, I can already ride, I don't need lessons. I have ridden loads and loads of times and I can do jumping and cantering and everything!"

"Well," Hester said, her patient tone slipping a little, "even the best riders have lessons. I'm sure you'll learn a lot from listening to Issie and Stella and Kate. When it comes to horses we can always learn more, can't we?"

Kelly-Anne didn't look at all convinced by this. "I knew this camp would be useless," she muttered as she stomped back to the horse truck to grab her bag.

Stella watched her go and then leant over and whispered to Issie and Kate, "There's always a Natasha Tucker in every group, isn't there?" The three girls exploded in a fit of giggles and had to rather unprofessionally hide in the tack room and pull themselves together while Hester led the young riders through the stables to Aidan's cottage to show them where they would be sleeping.

There was one room for the girls and the other bedroom was for George and Arthur. The girls had claimed that the sleeping arrangements were unfair as there were six of them in one room and only George and Arthur in the other. But then again, none of the girls actually wanted to move in and share George and Arthur's room. "Boy germs!" Lucy had shrieked, so that was the end of that complaint. That left the lumpy sofa in the living room. "For the dorm room monitor," Hester explained. "The girls are going to take turns staying out here at the cottage to keep an eye on you all."

This was news to Issie, Stella and Kate. It also didn't go down very well with the Blackthorn riders. "We don't need babysitting, you know," George said, clearly insulted by the idea.

That afternoon was pronounced "free time". Issie and Aidan gave the riders a tour of the farm, introducing them to Hester's performing animals. The younger riders stayed back to feed the goats, the rabbits and the chickens while the others went with Aidan to find racquets for the dilapidated old tennis court and fishing lines for catching eels in the duck pond by the cottage.

After dinner that night – big platters of spaghetti with tomato sauce and cheese cooked by Kate and Stella – it was time to relax before the first full day of riding tomorrow.

"You can watch TV until 9.30 then it's lights out," said Hester sternly. "We have early nights at the farm because we need to get up early too. You must all be back here dressed and ready for breakfast by 7 a.m."

There was a groan from George at this and Kelly-Anne looked sulky as usual, but the others seemed cheery enough as they stacked their plates and headed back down the hill for their first night in the cottage dormitory.

Issie was just about to get changed for bed herself when Aunt Hester knocked on the door of her room.

"Would you mind taking the first shift down at the dorm tonight, Issie?" she said. "I know the cottage is perfectly safe, but I think it's a good idea to have you there to make sure our guests are all right. Just for the first night at least. I know I'm a bit of a worry wart…"

"Sure, Aunty Hess," Issie grinned. "I'll look after them."

Issie stepped out on to the back verandah with her sleeping bag rolled up under her arm. She pulled on her boots and switched on her torch. It was funny how much darker the night was when you were in the countryside, she thought. No city lights, just the moonlight and the stars and the white beam of her torchlight as she walked across the lawn towards the cottage.

The lights were already out in the cottage. But as Issie

approached, she could see the flicker of a flame, possibly a candle, burning in the kitchen.

That's weird, she thought. Hester would never leave a candle on at night – it was too dangerous. What were those kids up to? As she came up to the front door of the cottage Issie was about to turn the handle, but something made her hesitate. Instead, she crept to the left of the door where a small, low window meant that she could see into the living room inside. It was hard for her eyes to adjust and Issie had to press her nose up against the glass to see in.

At first, she could hardly believe what she was seeing. Sitting there in the middle of the room, cross-legged in a circle around the candle flame, were the eight young riders. Their heads were shrouded in blankets so that they looked a bit like medieval monks. One by one, as if taking part in a mystical ceremony, they were picking up the candle and passing it to each other. Finally, the candle had travelled all the way around the circle until it came into the hands of George, who put it back down on the floor. George gave a wicked smile and looked at the two youngest children, Lucy and Sophie. The girls looked completely terrified. Issie couldn't hear what he was saying, but as George spoke Sophie looked like she might cry.

George looked at her with a devilish grin and then he blew out the candle! The cottage was now pitch-black! Issie couldn't stand it any longer. She had seen enough. She burst through the door and there were shrieks and screams from the startled kids inside as she switched on the light.

"What are you doing?" George squeaked.

"I came to check on you," Issie said, trembling. "And it's just as well!" She looked around the room at the frightened faces. "Now, who's going to tell me... what's going on?"

CHAPTER 6

Issie looked around the room at the faces of the terrified young riders. "Why are you all sitting here in the dark? What are you doing?"

They sat there mutely. No one was willing to answer. Issie looked at George, who had blown out the candle and was still holding on to it, looking the guiltiest of all of them.

"George?" Issie said. "Do you want to tell me what's going on here?"

"It was Arthur's idea!" George blurted out. "He started it!"

"Did not!" Arthur snapped back.

"Started what?" demanded Issie.

George hesitated. "We've been telling ghost stories,"

he said. "It was a competition to see who could tell the scariest one."

"Trisha is winning so far!" added Kitty. "She told that one about the hand with the hook, you know, in the forest, when they hear the tapping on the roof of the car? And then they find the hook stuck in the door?"

"That story was so lame!" Kelly-Anne groaned. "I never wanted to do stupid ghost stories in the first place. They're for babies."

"You're just in a sulk cos no one was scared of your story!" George shot back. Lucy and Sophie, the youngest ones in the group, were silent during all of this, huddled together in the corner under a blanket.

"Are you girls OK?" Issie asked. "Is this too scary for you?"

"No way!" Sophie grinned. "I love ghost stories!"

"We told the one about the bloody fingers!" beamed Lucy.

"Can you tell us one, Issie?" Tina asked.

"Go on!" Trisha begged.

"No," Issie said firmly. "It's lights out time. It's too late to be up telling ghost stories."

"But it's only ten o'clock; it's not even late!" Sophie said.

"Just one story and then we'll go to bed," added Tina. There was a murmur of agreement from the circle.

Issie sighed. "OK then. But after I tell you a story, everyone has to go to bed and straight to sleep, OK?"

Lucy and Sophie made a space in the circle between them and Issie nudged her way into it.

"Wait!" Arthur said, leaping up to grab the matches so that he could relight the candle. Then he switched off the light and the cottage was once again in darkness apart from a flickering flame.

Issie pulled a spare blanket up over her head like a hood, took the candle from Arthur and sat silently for a moment, the soft glow of the flame illuminating her face. "You won't have heard this ghost story before," she said in a low voice, "because what I'm about to tell you isn't a story at all. It is absolutely real. And it happened right here at Blackthorn Farm." She paused. "Are you sure you are brave enough to hear it?"

"Yes!" George and Arthur were both desperate for Issie to begin.

"Have you ever heard of the Grimalkin?" Issie asked. They all shook their heads. "The Grimalkin was a giant black cat that roamed the hills of Gisborne," Issie continued. "When I first heard the stories about him, they said he had escaped from the circus or the zoo and was living in the hills, wild and dangerous. Of course, no one really believed in him. They didn't think he was real. But I knew he was real because I saw him."

"Did you really?" Kitty said. "How big was he?"

"Big enough to eat a horse," said Issie. "The first time I saw him was just outside this cottage," she continued, "walking along the railings of the cattle pens. I could see him in the moonlight; he was jet black with this tail that was at least two metres long…"

"You're making this up to scare us!" Kelly-Anne objected.

Issie looked at her with a steely gaze. "I am not. You can ask Aunty Hess when you see her in the morning if you like."

"Shut up, Kelly-Anne!" George snapped. "The rest of us want to hear about the Grimalkin."

Issie had the sense to spare them the really gory details of that awful night when she and Aidan had found Meadow's body. The big black cat had killed the calf by slashing its throat with its powerful claws. Issie still had nightmares about poor Meadow, lying there with her rust and white coat soaked with blood. There was no need to give Sophie and Lucy nightmares too.

Huddled under their blankets, the Blackthorn Riders hung on Issie's every word. There was an audible groan of dismay when she finally finished her story and switched the lights back on.

"Was that all really true?" Tina asked. Issie nodded.

"Do you think there are still Grimalkins out there?" Lucy said, peering out at the blackness beyond the window.

"No, the Grimalkin is gone. I saw the ranger kill him. There's nothing out there now." Issie looked at the tired faces surrounding her in the candlelight. "OK, bedtime then," she said, shooing the riders out of the living room so that she could set up her bed on the sofa. "Let's go!"

"I told you we don't need a babysitter," George grumbled.

"What?"

"Yeah," Tina and Trisha agreed. "Please, Issie. We want to stay down here by ourselves. We don't need anyone to look after us."

Issie looked at the lumpy sofa. It was barely long enough for her to fit on and it looked horribly uncomfortable. She had to admit she would rather be in her enormous double bed back at the manor.

"OK," she said reluctantly. "But I need all of you to

get into bed before I go." There was a groan from George and Arthur, but no one argued with Issie this time.

As she switched out the bedroom lights she heard Lucy's voice in the darkness.

"Issie?"

"Yes, Lucy?"

"You know how we asked you to tell us a ghost story."

"Uh-huh."

"Well, that wasn't really a ghost story at all, was it? I mean, the Grimalkin wasn't actually a ghost. He was real."

"I suppose so," Issie said.

"Do you know any real ghost stories?" Lucy asked. "With proper ghosts in them?"

"Yeah, I do," Issie said.

"Will you tell us them?" asked Lucy.

"Maybe. But not tonight, Lucy. Go to sleep."

As Issie walked through the kitchen towards the cottage door she switched on her torch and swept the room, making one last check of the house before stepping outside into the cool night air and locking the door behind her.

The torch beam picked out a circle of light on the damp grass in front of her feet as she walked back across the lawn towards the main house. It wasn't far to walk.

All she had to do was wind her way between the trees behind the cottage and then cross the vast, sloping back lawn to the main house. She could see the back verandah light shining ahead of her, acting as a beacon guiding her way.

As she walked Issie thought about Lucy and how she wanted a "proper ghost story". She remembered Lucy's question, "Do you know any real ghost stories?" *Yeah*, Issie thought, *I really do*. Should she have told Lucy and the others about Mystic? There had been times when Issie felt desperate to tell someone about him, like she was going to burst if she kept her pony a secret any longer. For a moment in that room tonight she had considered telling the kids her own true story. She wanted to tell them that ghosts could truly be real – that Mystic was dead, but he was still with her somehow. He had come back to her, not as a ghost, but as flesh and blood, like a real horse. He was her horse and he always would be.

Issie wanted to tell them. But something stopped her. She was suddenly filled with the enormous weight of the dark truth that she held within her. At that moment she realised that Mystic wasn't something you could tell kids as a bedtime story. The sacred bond she shared with the grey gelding was too special to be turned into a campfire tale. Mystic had been her best friend. Now he was like her guardian angel. He was her secret and she shared it with no one – that was the way it had to be.

Issie had been so deep in thought that she was halfway across the lawn before she noticed the noise. In fact, even when she did finally notice it, she wasn't really sure whether she had actually heard something. Was it her turn to imagine ghosts now? No! There it was again! The noise sounded a bit like the crunching of branches underfoot. It was as if something or someone were following her. Issie spun around, shining her torch beam in a circle. Then she stopped and trained the beam on the garden to her right, where she thought the noise was coming from.

Issie kept her torch pointed on the garden. There! In the shadows. She could have sworn she saw a branch move. She shone the torch on the spot, but whatever it was had gone. She tried to listen again, but all she could hear was her own heart beating. All those ghost stories were getting the better of her!

Then she heard the rustling sound again. Closer this time. It was coming from behind the trees just beside her. She could hear branches crackling as something moved through the undergrowth.

"Is there someone there?" She could feel her palms sweating. "This isn't funny!" Issie's pulse quickened. She thought about what Lucy had said back at the cottage, about there being another Grimalkin. Maybe she was right. How did Issie know there had only been one? Ohmygod, what if...

Out of the shadows now a dark shape came towards her across the lawn. As it loomed closer Issie shone the torch beam directly at the creature. Not a black cat as Issie had feared, but a chestnut and white skewbald pony.

"Comet?" Issie groaned. "Comet! How did you get out?" Issie already knew the answer. Sure enough, when she led the skewbald back to his paddock she found the gate was still shut tight. Comet, must have jumped.

"One metre fifty!" Issie whistled. "And in the dark too!" She turned to face Comet, who was looking extremely pleased with himself.

"Comet!" Issie said firmly. "You have to stop this. No more jumping out or Aunty Hess is bound to put you back in the loose boxes. And you wouldn't like that, would you?"

For a moment there, Issie fancied that Comet actually understood her. The skewbald pony looked at her with sorrowful, deep brown eyes, as if to say, *Sorry, it won't happen again.*

Issie couldn't help but giggle at his apologetic expression. "OK then," she said, opening the gate, "I'm giving you one last chance." As Issie released her grip on his halter the skewbald trotted off merrily across the paddock. Issie shook her head as she watched him go. Would he still be there by the morning? Hester would have a blue fit if he jumped out again. Maybe Issie should just give up and lock him up now in the loose boxes herself?

Issie trained her torchlight on the paddock, searching for Comet. And then she felt her pulse quicken as she caught something unexpected in the beam. There was another horse in the paddock with Comet! She had only caught a glimpse of him for just a moment, but she was sure of it! Searching frantically in the darkness, she waved the torch beam back and forth trying to find the horse again. There! He was standing next to Comet. She could see him quite clearly this time. She could even make out the grey dapples of his coat, the flash of silver mane. Her heart leapt as she realised who it was.

"Mystic?" Issie called out. "Is that you?" She held the torch with both hands to keep it steady, worried that if the light beam slipped away even for a moment then the grey horse would disappear and she wouldn't be able to find him again.

"Hey, boy?" Issie called out. She was close now, almost there… Issie kept expecting the horse to vanish, but he was there. He stood perfectly still in the torchlight and his black eyes shone back at her. He was waiting for her. She reached out a hand and touched the thick, coarse strands of Mystic's silver mane. "Hey, boy," she breathed softly. "It's good to see you."

Mystic nickered softly as Issie stepped closer to him and leant against his shoulder, wrapping her arms around the pony's neck, burying her face deep in the grey pony's mane as she hugged him tight.

Their embrace was interrupted by the sound of Comet moving behind her. From the moment Issie had met Comet she had sensed there was something special about the skewbald pony. Maybe Mystic sensed it too? Certainly, it was no coincidence that Mystic was here. It meant something.

"Are you here to keep an eye on him?" Issie murmured to Mystic. "Maybe you can convince him to stay in his paddock for the night for once?"

The grey gelding seemed to acknowledge his new task as Comet's babysitter. He gave a soft nicker at Issie's instructions, then wheeled about and trotted off into the darkness, fading out of her sight. Comet raised his head up as Mystic disappeared, then he trotted after him, following the grey horse across the paddock.

Issie grinned. If anyone could help control a wayward pony like Comet, it had to be Mystic. She stood there for a moment longer in the dark, flashing the beam of her torch where the horses had been. But they were too far away for her torch to penetrate now, lost in the pitch black at the far side of the field.

"G'night, Mystic," Issie murmured. "Keep him safe, OK?"

Issie walked back to the manor deep in thought. As much as she was thrilled to see Mystic again, her horse's appearance had left her worried. If Mystic was here then it meant trouble of some kind.

As she took off her boots and put her torch down on the table by the back door, she felt a chill run down her spine. She walked through the kitchen and was about to head upstairs to her room when something made her stop. There was a light on in the small alcove off the kitchen that Hester used as her office. Issie tiptoed in her socks across the parquet floor and peered through the door of the alcove. Her aunt was hunched over her desk, a mound of paperwork stacked in front of her. Hester took off her reading glasses to rub her eyes and as she did so she caught sight of Issie standing behind her. Startled, she dropped her glasses and then scrambled to pick them up again so she could see who was standing in the doorway.

"Issie! I thought you were sleeping at the cottage. You gave me quite a turn!" Hester looked tense.

"The kids threw me out. They're fine. I came back here to sleep," Issie explained. "What are you doing, Aunty Hess?"

Hester readjusted her spectacles. "A bit of book-keeping – the farm accounts, that sort of thing." Issie looked at the mound of bills on the writing desk in front of her aunt.

"Is it true, what Aidan said? You might have to sell the farm?"

Hester took her glasses back off and rubbed her eyes a second time. "Yes, well, Aidan's jumping the gun a bit. I'm not selling it just yet. We have enough money in the emergency coffers to see us through for another month. Perhaps two months if we scrimp."

"What will happen after that?"

"Mortgagee sale, I expect. I want to take the horses with me, but where would we go? I won't be able to take them all. Or the other animals – or Aidan for that matter."

"How much money do you need?"

"A windfall of around $25,000 is all it would take," Hester said. "I've been buying lottery tickets so that's bound to pay off soon I should imagine."

She looked at Issie with tired eyes. "I am doing everything I can, favourite niece. And I cannot tell you how much it means to me that you are here to help me." Hester smiled weakly. "Anyway, I'm sure we'll muddle through. So stop standing in the doorway looking at me with those sorrowful eyes. You look like one of my jersey cows with that expression!" She waved Issie out of the office. "Off you go to bed and stop worrying! You have a rowdy group of riders to teach in the morning."

Issie stood there for a moment longer but her aunt was firm. "I said goodnight, Isadora."

"G'night, Aunty Hess."

Upstairs in her room, Issie lay on her bed and stared at the painting of Avignon on her wall above the fireplace. Why was Mystic here? The grey horse wanted to help in some way, but how could he? Even Issie couldn't help. What Blackthorn Farm really needed was money – and she didn't have $25,000.

CHAPTER 7

At breakfast the next morning Hester dropped another bombshell.

"I've just had a call from old Bill Stokes who lives down by Preacher's Cove," she told the girls. "There's been an accident. There was a landslide in the cove and Bill has found six of my sheep trapped on a ledge with no way out. He said they're very distressed, must have been stuck there all night. I told him I'd drive down there with Aidan this morning and winch them up to safety with the horse truck."

"This morning?" Issie squeaked. "But, Aunty Hess, it's the first day of the riding school."

"I know it's leaving you in the lurch," Hester said, "but I've got no choice, Issie. Those poor animals are in a frightful state – it can't wait."

Hester saw the worried looks on the girls' faces. "You've got your lesson plan. I'm sure you'll be fine."

Issie wasn't so sure. "George, and Kelly-Anne will be the worst," she muttered as they walked down the driveway to the stables. "They're too busy picking fights with each other to listen to us. And Kelly-Anne thinks she knows everything."

"You have to treat them just like horses," Stella insisted. "Don't show any fear or they'll pick up on it."

"You're right," Kate said. "You just have to take control of that lesson, Stella, and show them you're in charge."

"Me?" Stella stared at Kate as if she was crazy. "Not me! I'm not teaching them. You are! You're the head instructor, Kate – you're the one with the most experience and everything. Those riders are bound to listen to you."

"You're kidding!" said Kate.

"Go on!" Stella grinned. "Issie and I will be there right behind you to back you up! Won't we, Issie?"

"Yep!" Issie grinned. They were right behind Kate too – hiding behind her and giggling as they made her go first through the stable doors to meet the riders.

"Right!" Kate said, reluctantly taking command and addressing the eight pupils sitting on the hay bales. The riders were dressed in their jods and boots ready to get started. "Before we even begin to think about getting on our ponies, what do we need to do first?" Eight faces stared blankly back at her.

"We have to catch them of course!" Kate smiled. "Follow me to the tack room." She led the eight riders into the tack room. Hung neatly on the walls on named pegs were rows of halters and bridles. "Now who can tell me which one is a halter and which one is a bridle?" Kate asked.

Trisha and Tina's hands shot up. "The one with a bit and reins is the bridle. The halter doesn't have a bit. You use the halter to catch them and tie them up while you're grooming and stuff," Trisha said.

"Very good!" said Kate. "Now can you all please pick up the halter of the horse that you'll be riding, grab a carrot each out of the feed bins and let's go catch our ponies." This proved to be easier said than done.

"We didn't have to catch our own ponies at our last riding school," Lucy said. "They had them all ready for us to ride when we arrived."

"I can't undo the strap!" Sophie groaned, struggling

to pull the stiff leather through the buckle.

Meanwhile, Stella was busy with George, who had managed to put a halter on Diablo, but had somehow got it upside down and couldn't figure out what he had done wrong.

"Is anyone else having problems?" Kate asked. She looked over at Kelly-Anne, who had managed to get her halter done up but had the lead rope wrapped tightly around her hand. "Always hold the lead rope at the shank and don't wrap it around your hand like that!" Kate called out to her. "What you're doing is dangerous. If Julian bolts on you and the rope tightens, you could end up getting dragged along by your pony or with a broken finger."

"I know what I'm doing!" Kelly-Anne snapped back. "Stop being so bossy." Still, she unwrapped the rope that was twirled around her hand and held it correctly the way Kate had shown her.

"Has everyone got their halters on?" Kate called out. "Right. Let's lead them back to the loose boxes."

Once they were inside, the riders were all shown how to tie a slip knot to tether the ponies and then Kate led them to the tack room.

"Your gear should be stacked next to the nameplate of your horse," Kate explained. "You've each got a bucket with your own grooming kit. You should have a hoof pick, a curry comb, a sweat scraper, a sponge, a dandy brush, body brush and a mane comb each. Can you all check your kits?" The riders all dug about in their buckets and tried to identify the various bits of their grooming kit.

"Your saddles and bridles always go in the same place in the tack room and your racks are name-tagged with your pony's name," Kate continued. "There will be a prize each week for the person who keeps their tack and kit the tidiest and cleanest…"

There was a groan from Kelly-Anne at the idea of cleaning gear. "Are we actually going to do any riding today? You want us to clean the ponies and stuff? It's like we're doing your work for you!"

"Grooming your horse is an important skill you need to learn," Kate said. "Can anyone tell me why we bother to groom before we ride?"

"To make our horses look pretty?" Lucy offered.

"Yes, but what else?" There was silence. "Grooming a horse isn't just about making them look nice," Kate said. "It also gives you a chance to check for injuries, to see if your horse has a saddle sore or if there's a stone stuck in a shoe. Even if you are in a screaming hurry, you should always give your horse a quick groom all over to check that it is OK."

"Now," Kate said, "when I call your name, can you come up please and grab your bucket of brushes and your tack. And remember to carry the saddles with your arms through the gullet the way we showed you."

Lucy and Sophie were both struggling to carry their own saddles, so Issie helped them to lug their gear back to the loose boxes.

"Will you help us put the saddles on too?" Sophie asked. "The thing is, when we ride at the riding school they always have our ponies ready for us."

"So you've never even groomed a horse before? Or put on a saddle and bridle?" Issie was stunned. "That's awful. Horses aren't just furry bicycles that you can park up at the end of the day, you know!" The girls giggled nervously at this.

"Come on," Issie smiled at them, "it won't take you long to learn. I'll give you a grooming lesson right now."

And so Issie showed Sophie and Lucy how to groom their ponies, starting at the head and working back towards the tail, using the body brush on the soft parts of the horse where the saddle went, and the dandy brush to scrub the mud off their ponies' hocks.

"I think I'm hurting him!" Sophie wailed as she snagged her mane comb in Pippen's thick grey mane.

"He's fine," Issie reassured her. "Ponies' manes really aren't very sensitive."

Lucy, meanwhile, was trying to pick out Molly's hooves, but kept getting nervous and shrieking every time Molly tried to help by obediently picking up her feet. It took forever for Sophie and Lucy to get Molly and Pippen groomed, and even longer to saddle up.

"Are you lot ready yet?" Stella stuck her head over the stall door. "It's almost lunchtime and we haven't even started riding!"

Eventually, all eight riders had their ponies tacked up, their helmets on and their stirrups at the right length, and they were riding around the arena.

"Keep two horse lengths between you and the horse in front of you," Kate called out as the riders walked around. "And trot on! Rising trot, everyone. Come on, Arthur, keep Glennie moving!"

"He won't go!" Kelly-Anne, who was bouncing about in the saddle like a sack of potatoes with wobbly hands, was having trouble getting Julian to trot.

"Just put your legs, try and keep your hands still and don't jag him in the mouth. He'll move forward," Kate instructed. But Kelly-Anne wasn't having any of it.

Kate, Issie and Stella were forced to watch in horror as Kelly-Anne lifted her legs up and away from her pony's sides and then brought them down again with a bang, giving Julian an almighty boot in the sides and digging her heels hard into his ribcage!

Julian, not used to being kicked in the tummy, got such a shock that he bolted forward into a frantic canter and Kelly-Anne, who hadn't been expecting him to move quite so suddenly, let out a squeal as she lost her balance. Julian, realising his rider was in trouble, came to a sudden stop and Kelly-Anne flew forward, out of the saddle and landed smack flat on her bottom in the middle of the arena in front of the entire ride, whereupon she immediately burst into floods of tears.

"Well, that's a brilliant start," Stella muttered to Issie under her breath as Kate rushed forward to help Kelly-Anne up, grabbing Julian's reins with one hand.

"Are you OK?" Kate asked as she picked Kelly-Anne up off the ground.

"I'm fine. He's a stupid horse. I was just making him go!" Kelly-Anne said defiantly.

"That's not how you make a horse go!" said Kate.

"Well, that's how I do it," Kelly-Anne sniffed.

"I can see that!" said Kate. She turned to Issie and Stella. "I think we'd better run through some basic rules before we even try the rest of them at a canter."

"Uh-huh," Issie nodded.

"I think I saw a whiteboard and a felt pen in the tack room," Stella said. "It might help if we write them down!"

When Stella returned a few moments later with the whiteboard, she had already written a title across the top: The Blackthorn Farm Riding School's Five Commandments

"Umm, Stella? Aren't there supposed to be ten commandments?" Kate asked.

"They'll never remember ten!" Stella said. "Five is enough to start with."

"OK," Issie said to the riders. "Can anyone tell me the first rule? What is the most important thing when you are riding?"

"Ummm, being nice to your pony?" Sophie said.

"Excellent!" Issie said. "What else?"

A hand shot up from one of the other riders. "Ummm, don't kick?" Tina said.

Pretty soon everyone had their hands up (except for Kelly-Anne, who was still in a sulk about being told off)

and in no time at all Stella had written up her list.

The Blackthorn Farm Riding School's Five Commandments

1. Always treat your pony with kindness. A good rider makes their pony happy.
2. Never kick your pony to make him go. A squeeze is enough.
3. Never yank on the reins to make him stop. A squeeze is enough too!
4. Do not flap your arms and legs. You are a rider, not a chicken.
5. A good rider is quiet in the saddle. Keep your heels down, your eyes up and your hands steady.

The lesson was short and simple that morning. The girls made their pupils clamber around in the saddle doing round-the-world, before swinging their legs to the front and the back to do heel clicks. Then they played the Mounting Game. Stella popped a series of yellow, red and blue feed bins on the ground. The riders had to dismount and pick up an object out of their grooming kits before remounting, trotting up to the bin and throwing the items in one by one. They had to dismount again to get the next piece until their grooming kits were empty and the bins were full. They finished the morning session by making all the riders show them the perfect position in the saddle.

"You need to think of a straight line from your ear to your elbow to your heel," Issie said as she adjusted Lucy's leg so that it was back against the girth. "You must maintain that vertical line at all times."

"Can anyone tell me what other straight line you must keep at all times?" Stella asked.

"Umm, is it the elbow to the bit?" asked Tina.

"That's right! Imagine a line straight from the horse's bit to your elbow – that means your hands are in the right position."

"That's easy," Kelly-Anne snorted.

"Yes, but you haven't actually tried moving yet, have you?" said Stella. "It's easy to maintain the perfect position when you're just sitting there, but wait until you start trotting – or cantering!"

"Yeah, you had the perfect position until you fell off on your bum!" George grinned at Kelly-Anne.

"George!" Issie cautioned him. "Everyone falls off.

Horsey people have a saying: you have to fall off seven times before you are a real rider."

"Anyway," Kate looked at her watch, "I think we've all had enough for the morning. It's lunchtime. Let's get these ponies untacked."

It took almost as long for Lucy and Sophie to unsaddle the horses as it had taken for them to tack up. As Issie helped them, she drilled the girls on their general knowledge.

"We'll play Pony Questions," Issie told them. "Let's see who can be the first one to give me the right answer. Are you ready?" The girls nodded.

"What colour is a piebald?"

"Ohh!" Sophie's hand shot up. "Black and white!"

"Excellent! And what is another name for a piebald? The name the Americans use? We should really use it for Diablo because he's a Quarter Horse…"

"A paint?" Sophie guessed.

"That's right!" said Issie. "Next question then. Who can point to their horse's fetlock?" Lucy pointed to the bottom of her pony's leg.

"Very good, Lucy!"

The girls loved Pony Questions and were begging Issie for more as they walked back up the road from the stables. When Issie finally arrived in the kitchen she found Aidan valiantly defending the last piece of chicken pie for her.

"Are the sheep all OK?" asked Issie.

"They're fine," Aidan said. "We got them all up the bank again and then Hester dropped me back here so I could help with lunch. She's gone to help Bill Stokes fix the fence – the landslide took out a whole section along the Coast Road."

Aidan passed her the pie. "George and Arthur both wanted to eat your piece," he explained. "You'd have been forced to survive on one of Hester's leftover scones."

"Ughh!" Issie took the plate gratefully. "Thanks! I'm so starving. It's been a tough morning."

"Want to sit outside?" Aidan asked. They walked out to the back verandah and sat down on the steps that led to the garden with their lunch plates on their laps.

"So how are your students?" Aidan wanted to know.

"They can all ride," Issie said. "Well, I'm not so sure about Kelly-Anne, but the rest of them can. They don't know the first thing about ponies though. It's like they've had everything done for them."

"You'll sort them out," Aidan said. "In three weeks time they'll all be riding like experts."

"I don't know about that," Issie groaned. "They're probably desperate for the weekend to come so that they can go home and get away from us bossing them around!"

Aidan shifted about uncomfortably and looked down at his feet. "Yeah, I was thinking about that, about the weekend. I know you've got lots to do during the week with the riding school and everything, but I was thinking maybe this Saturday, when you're not working, we could pack a picnic and go for a ride. With the film work drying up I've had some spare time to build a cross-country course across the farm. It's pretty basic, but there are about ten jumps and some of them are quite good. We could ride the horses over a couple of them and then go for a swim at Lake Deepwater…"

"That sounds cool!" Issie said, "I'll tell Stella and Kate and…"

"No!" Aidan blurted out. "I meant just the two of us. You know, like on a date." Aidan looked at her and as his piercing blue eyes locked with her own Issie suddenly felt her heart hammering in her chest, pounding so loud that she barely heard the words that came next.

"Issie… do you want to go out with me?"

CHAPTER 8

Aidan's words hung in the air. He had asked her out!

"Aidan, I, umm…" Issie didn't know what to say.

"Never mind," Aidan said, looking uncomfortable. "I was just thinking that… look, it's OK. You don't have to…"

"No," Issie said. "I mean, no, I want to. I mean yes. My answer is yes. Yes, Aidan, I'd love to."

"Great!" Aidan looked relieved. "Great! I…"

"Hey, you two!" Stella was suddenly right there behind them with her lunch plate in her hands. "Is this a private conversation or can anyone join in?"

"Actually…" Issie began, but it was too late as Stella sat down, squeezing herself in between Issie and Aidan.

"Come on, make a bit of room!"

"Here, you can have my seat," Aidan said. "I'd better go anyway. I'll see you back at the stables in an hour, OK?" Aidan stood up to leave and Stella took his place.

"So?" Stella said to Issie as they watched him walk off. "How are things with Aidan then?"

Issie felt herself blushing hot pink. "He just asked me out."

"Ohmygod!"

"We're going to go on a picnic to the lake on Saturday."

"But it's only Tuesday. That's ages away!"

"I know!" Issie groaned. "I wish it was Saturday now. It's going to feel like forever."

"What did he say exactly?" Stella said. "I want to know all the details!"

"We're going riding to try out this new cross-country course and go swimming at the lake."

"Cool," Stella said. "I'll tell Kate. She loves cross-country. What time are we going?"

"Ummm…" Issie didn't know what to say. "It was just going to be me and Aidan."

Stella's smile faded. "Oh."

"But I can tell him!" Issie said. "If you and Kate want to come too, we could all go together…"

"No," Stella said. "That's OK. It's a date. You don't need us tagging along." She gave Issie a disappointed look. "You go with Aidan. We'll go together another time."

The girls hardly saw Aidan or Hester at all that week. Hot on the heels of the drama with the stranded sheep, Hester received a call from Ranger Cameron. He'd spotted a Blackthorn mare running wild with a young foal at foot, up on the back ridge behind the lake. Hester and Aidan set off to try to catch her, leaving the girls in charge of the school once more.

"You'll be fine. You girls know what you're doing," Hester tried to reassure Issie. "I'm on my mobile if you need me. Just keep working your way through the lesson plan we made up."

According to the lesson plan, Wednesday was games day. Issie, Stella and Kate organised a barrel race, flag race, bending poles and an egg and spoon competition. Tina and Trisha, who turned out to be complete and utter daredevils, won every single competition between them – except for the egg and spoon race, which Arthur won on Glennie. Everyone was suspicious that his egg had been stuck to the spoon with chewing gum, but Arthur insisted he hadn't cheated.

Thursday was spent on basic flatwork and pony care. Friday morning was flatwork too and all the riders were excited because they'd been told they'd finally be doing some jumping in the afternoon.

"Has anyone used cavaletti before?" Kate asked the riders as they gathered in the centre of the arena after lunch. The eight riders all shook their heads. "Cavaletti are great for developing your pony's gymnastics. Can anyone tell me what that means?" Kate asked.

George sniggered. "What like doing forward rolls and cartwheels and stuff?"

"No, I mean gymnastic jumping," Kate said. "We're going to do what showjumpers refer to as 'gridwork'." She walked to the middle of the arena where two rows of white painted cavaletti were lined up.

"Cavaletti are not big jumps," she explained. "Their purpose is to teach you how to stay balanced and get a rhythm going. Plus, they'll make your ponies learn to think and lift their feet. Can everyone get into two-point position like I showed you please?" said Kate. "And take your stirrups up to jumping length first. We're only going to be jumping very small cavaletti today so two holes should do it."

Kate, Issie and Stella worked their way down the row of riders, checking everyone's jumping position.

"In two-point position we stand up in our stirrups a little and balance on our knees and our bodies tilt forward," Kate explained. "Let's try to get our positions sorted in the arena without jumps first." She made the riders trot around the school. "Everyone sitting in their normal position, excellent... Now... two-point!" she shouted and the riders all tilted forward. "And back again!" Kate instructed.

"My legs are getting tired," Kelly-Anne whined.

"You haven't even started jumping yet!" said Kate. "You'll get used to it. Put all your weight into your heels, balance on your knees. Now we're going to try our two-point over the cavaletti. Tina, you go first." Tina trotted towards the white jumps.

"Look up!" Kate shouted. "Never, ever look down at the bottom of the jump. If you look down then your horse will stop. You must look where you want to go – up and over the fence."

"That was cool!" Tina was beaming from ear to ear as she finished.

"You're next, Kelly-Anne," Kate called. "Hurry up.

Kelly-Anne! You must look up!" As Julian approached the cavaletti Kelly-Anne ignored Kate's advice. Instead, her eyes went straight down to the ground where the first pole was. Julian was a well-schooled pony and there was no way he was going to jump a cavaletti if his rider was looking at the ground. He didn't know what else to do so he stopped dead in front of the poles.

Kelly-Anne let out a squeal, "Stupid pony! Get up!" And before anyone could stop her she had lifted her riding crop up high and brought it down hard on the brown pony's rump. "Jump, you pig!" she yelled. Julian didn't have a clue what was wrong. Why was this girl hitting him? He gave an indignant snort and leapt to one side as Kelly-Anne squealed and struck him again. This time she brought the stick down hard on his shoulder. Julian was panicking now; the whites of his eyes were showing as he backed away from the cavaletti.

"Kelly-Anne, stop it!" Issie rushed forward. "He doesn't know what you want him to do. You're just scaring him!"

"He's a stupid, stupid pony!" Kelly-Anne said. She was so furious, so lost in her anger that Issie could see that any drop of common sense she might have had was quickly disappearing, consumed by her fury.

"Give me the whip, Kelly-Anne," Issie said coolly.

Kelly-Anne didn't respond. She glared back at Issie, who reached out and grabbed the riding crop out of her hand. "I said, give me the whip!" she snapped. "And don't ever think about riding like that again – or I'll have you sent home from this school and you won't be back."

"I was just teaching him who's boss," Kelly-Anne insisted.

"You weren't teaching him anything except how to be afraid of a girl who doesn't know how to ride," Issie snapped back.

Kelly-Anne looked at Issie as if she was going to explode. Then she jumped down, threw Julian's reins at her and stormed off. "I don't want to ride him anyway," she fumed as she stomped towards the stables. "He's just a dumb learner's pony!"

"Shall I go after her and try to explain why what she did was wrong?" Stella asked as they watched Kelly-Anne flounce off.

"Leave her," Issie sighed. "Let's get on with the lesson. I'm going to tell Aunty Hess tonight. I won't put up with her treating Julian like that. It's got to stop now."

When Hester heard about Kelly-Anne's behaviour she agreed. "I've taken her aside and had a good talk to her," Hester told the girls as they set the table for dinner. "She's on a good behaviour bond. The riders are all going home first thing in the morning anyway, so that will give her the weekend to cool down. When she comes back to the school on Monday, I expect her to have a new attitude."

Apart from Kelly-Anne, who was now in a permanent sulk, everyone was in a cheery mood at dinner. Hester had defied the odds by turning out a decent meal for once, including a steak pie that was entirely edible.

"I have some news," she told the girls as they tucked gratefully into their unburnt dinner. "Tom Avery is coming to stay."

"What?" Issie just about choked on her pie in surprise.

"He called today and told me that he was planning to come down this weekend with Dan and Ben to prepare for the Horse of the Year. They were going to keep the horses at a stable near the showgrounds, but I suggested that they come here instead."

"Do we have enough room for them?" asked Issie.

"Of course. We've got loads of grazing and spare loose boxes. Tom says he and the boys were planning to camp in his horse truck, and now they won't have to. They can stay here at the house instead for the next fortnight. We have loads of room," said Hester. "Plus, Avery has offered to pay board and grazing costs for the ponies – and right now every bit helps."

"When do they get here?" asked Aidan, looking less than impressed at the idea of Dan turning up.

"Tomorrow lunchtime," Hester said. "So I'll need a bit of help first thing in the morning getting their rooms ready and preparing stalls for the two new ponies."

"But tomorrow is Saturday!" Issie blurted out. She was thrilled that her instructor and pony-club friends were coming to stay, but did it have to be tomorrow? She had been waiting all week for her date with Aidan and now there was no way she could leave the farm for the day.

"I'm sorry," Issie told Aidan when they took their dishes to the kitchen. "About the picnic, I mean."

"That's OK," said Aidan. "I figure we can still ride."

"What do you mean?"

"We've still got a couple of hours in the morning before they get here and there are no lessons going on in the arena," Aidan said. "What about if we saddle up Destiny and Stardust and do some showjumping training?"

"Really?" Issie felt her heart race. It had been ages since she did proper jumping.

"Sure, the cavaletti are already set up and I can build us a jumping course too," Aidan said. "That is… if you want to?"

"I do!" Issie said. Then she hesitated. "There's just one thing, Aidan. I don't want to ride Stardust. I want to ride Comet."

"Really?" Aidan was surprised. "Issie, Comet is pretty green. I've taken him over cross-country jumps when we've been out riding, and he's done a bit of gridwork over cavaletti, but Stardust has had far more proper schooling in the showjumping ring."

"I know," Issie said, "but he's a natural jumper, Aidan. I've seen him." She smiled. "He didn't need any training to learn how to jump out of his paddock, did he?"

Aidan grinned. "No… no, I guess he didn't."

Comet seemed to know that something exciting was happening the next morning when Issie arrived at the stables. The skewbald pony moved about anxiously in his stall as she entered.

"Easy, boy," Issie cooed softly under her breath as she slipped the bridle over his head and did up her own helmet straps, before slipping on her riding gloves. "Let's go."

In the arena Aidan and Destiny were already warming up. "I've set up a showjumping course," Aidan said, gesturing to a small circuit of jumps that he had built at the far end of the arena, "but I thought we should start with some cavaletti."

The two riders did exactly the same gridwork that the kids had been doing earlier that week, practising their positions and making the horses trot through the cavaletti. As she worked him over the cavaletti Issie couldn't help smiling at Comet. His confidence as he took the jumps was like nothing she had ever seen before. He was such a bold jumper – and such a show-off! Issie had to try not to giggle each time they finished and Comet gave a dramatic flick of his tail, a bit like a horsey version of a high-five, thrashing the air emphatically.

"You are funny, Comet!" Issie gave him a slappy pat on his glossy neck and turned to Aidan.

"He's going brilliantly, isn't he?" said Aidan. "They seem pretty well warmed up. Shall we try them over some proper jumps?"

The first fence in the course was parallel rails, the second was a hog's back, then you turned left to approach the double, which had just one stride between the fences and quite a decent spread on the last fence. The fifth and final fence was the biggest by far and was made up of blue and white painted rails with hay bales stacked underneath.

Issie and Aidan both dismounted to walk the course together. "The striding is pretty easy," Aidan said. "You have to turn quite sharply to take the hog's back after the parallel rails, and then there's one stride in between the first and second fence of the double."

Issie stood next to the hay bales. It was a big fence. The bales came all the way up past her waist almost to her chest.

"It's one metre twenty," Aidan said. "Destiny and I will be jumping this height at the Horse of the Year."

Issie nodded. She had jumped a fence the size of the hay bales loads of times before on Blaze, but never on Comet. She felt the butterflies in her tummy beginning to flutter. Cavaletti were all well and good, but what would the skewbald be like over such big jumps with a rider on his back?

"I'll go first, OK?" Aidan said.

Issie didn't know whether it made it better or worse that Destiny took the five fences so effortlessly. The black stallion positively flew over the double, barely bothering to even put in a stride, and took the hay bales at the end with ease for a clear round.

"Good lad!" Aidan gave Destiny a slappy pat on his broad black neck as he pulled the stallion up to a halt next to little Comet. "Do you want me to put the fences down for you before you go?" Aidan asked. The jumps were at the right height for a horse like Destiny who was sixteen-two, but for a little pony like Comet these were big fences.

As Issie eyed up the jumps, there was something about the way Comet danced and skipped beneath her that made her think he was almost trying to say, *I can do this! Let's go!*

"No. Leave them," Issie said. "I think we'll be OK."

When you watch horses showjumping on TV, they make it look so simple. Even the biggest fences seem to be no big deal. But when you are actually riding in the showjumping ring in real life, facing a massive fence made out of painted rails, it's quite a different story.

Issie had a brief moment as she turned Comet to begin her warm-up circle when she felt her nerve falter.

What if Comet didn't jump? If the pony suddenly stopped or swerved she might lose her balance and fall. She shook her head, as if trying to shake the bad thoughts out of her brain. She remembered what Avery had told her about staying positive and tried to imagine herself soaring cleanly over each fence.

"Steady, Comet," she said firmly. The skewbald was tense with anticipation. Issie tried to ride him into a steady canter as she approached the first fence. There was a moment, a couple of strides out from the jump, when it looked like Comet was going to refuse, but he simply put in an extra stride to get deeper into the fence and leapt it cleanly. He took the hog's back too with ease and put in a perfect stride between fence one and two of the double combination.

As they turned to face the hay bales Issie felt herself stiffen in the saddle and the butterflies returned. She looked down at Comet who was pulling like mad against her hands, filled with his own pure love of jumping, and she sat back in the saddle and let him go. Comet put in two huge canter strides, gathered himself up and absolutely flew over the hay bales, giving a high-spirited victory buck as he cantered away on the other side.

"Oh, well done, Comet!" Issie had a grin on her face a

mile wide as she pulled the skewbald to a stop and let go of the reins to give him a pat on both sides of his neck. "Good pony!" The sound of applause from the side of the arena made her look up.

"Excellent round!"

"Tom!" Issie was surprised to see her instructor standing there, clapping vigorously.

"That's quite the horse you've got there," Avery called out to her. "What's he called?"

"Comet," Issie said. "His name is Comet."

Avery ducked down, slipped between the rails of the fence and strode across the arena towards Issie and Comet. He ran his eyes over the horse, his face serious, clearly deep in thought. "Nice solid bone, strong hindquarters," Avery murmured as he assessed him, "and a scopey jump too. I haven't seen a pony jump like that in a very long time…" He looked up at Issie. "Well, it looks like I got here just in time."

"In time for what?"

"To start your training." Avery patted the skewbald's neck. "Issie, Comet is a superstar in the making. We'd better get cracking." He paused. "That is, if we're going to enter him in the Grand Prix at the Horse of the Year Show."

CHAPTER 9

Issie was stunned. Did Avery really think that Comet was good enough to jump at the Horse of the Year? Surely her instructor was joking?

"I'm completely serious," Avery insisted. "This pony is a natural athlete. I was watching him over those jumps and he's got a terrific bascule."

"What's a bascule?"

"A good jumper will stretch his neck out and tuck up his front feet over a fence so that he almost looks like a dolphin flying through the air," Avery explained. "That's called a bascule. It's absolutely crucial in a showjumper. Comet has it. With a little training to perfect his technique, that natural ability could be enough to earn him a clear round in the pony Grand Prix at the Horse of the Year. "

Issie vaulted down off Comet's back and landed on the ground beside her pony. The cheeky skewbald was listening intently with his ears pricked forward, as if he knew that Issie and her instructor were talking about him.

"He can clear any fence on the farm," Issie said as she told Avery about Comet's habit of jumping out of paddocks. "He's totally fearless!"

"Well," said Avery, "let's see if we can harness his natural talents. We've got two weeks before the Horse of the Year qualifying rounds to get some solid schooling in. I think the best plan is for you and Comet to join in on my jumping lessons with the boys." Avery saw Issie's uncertain expression. "Is there a problem?"

"It's just that I'm supposed to be working, Tom. I won't have time…"

"Don't worry," Avery said. "You can fit it in. Hester needs the arena during the day for her riding school anyway so I've agreed with her to use it in the evenings. We'll switch on the floodlights and have jumping practice after dinner each night. That means you'll have time to teach the school during the day – although you'll be pretty exhausted by the end of the day, I should imagine."

Issie grinned. "That sounds brilliant!"

"Where's my training squad got to anyway?" Avery looked over at the stables. "I asked those boys to put their horses away in the loose boxes ages ago. What is taking them so long?"

As he said this Dan and Ben emerged from the stables with halters in their hands. When Dan saw Issie his face lit up. He gave her a wave and began to run across the arena towards her. Then he caught sight of Aidan, who was still working Destiny around the showjumping course, and his expression suddenly turned dark.

Aidan had caught sight of Dan too and didn't look pleased to see him either. He took Destiny over one last fence and then pulled the stallion up and trotted back over to join the group.

"Aidan!" Avery said. "Good to see you again! You've got Destiny going very nicely."

"Thanks, Tom," said Aidan.

"You know Dan and Ben, don't you?" asked Avery.

"Yeah." Aidan reached down from his horse to shake hands with Ben and then put his hand out to Dan. Dan hesitated for a moment and then reluctantly took his hand and shook it as the boys exchanged a gruff hello.

"I was just asking Issie if she wanted to take part in Horse of the Year training in the evenings now that we're here," Avery told Aidan. "Do you want to join us too? We'll give the horses a day to settle in and then our first training session will be on Monday. "

"Absolutely," Aidan said. He stared directly at Dan. "If Issie is doing it then I'll definitely be there. I wouldn't miss it."

On Sunday night, when the Blackthorn Riders had returned from their weekend at home, everyone sat around the dinner table and discussed Avery's training sessions.

"What about us? Can Kate and I do it too?" asked Stella. "I mean," she added grumpily under her breath to Issie, "unless it's just you and Aidan, like a date." Issie felt the sting in Stella's comment, but Avery didn't notice the tension between the two girls.

"Absolutely," he agreed. "I'm sure Coco and Toby are both capable of jumping the heights we'll be doing at the training sessions if you girls both want to join in."

The younger riders seemed very excited by the idea of proper showjumping training.

"What about us?" Arthur asked. "Can we all come and watch?"

"I don't see why not – if that's OK with you, Hester?" Avery said.

"I think it's a great idea," Hester agreed. "We'll make sure we have an early dinner and then you can meet up at the arena. You'll learn a lot from watching other riders. I'm sure all of you will pick up some excellent technique tips."

Kelly-Anne looked doubtful about this. "I don't want to watch," she said. "I want to ride too." There was silence and then a giggle from some of the other kids.

"What?" Kelly-Anne glared at them. "I've done loads of showjumping and it's easy. I could totally compete at Horse of the Year if I had Comet instead of stupid old Julian!"

"No, you couldn't!" Arthur said.

"I could so!" Kelly-Anne snapped back.

"Gee, Kelly-Anne," George rolled his eyes. "You are such a fibber!"

"I am not!" Kelly-Anne's face was red with anger. "You don't know anything about horses anyway!" There were daggers in her eyes as she pushed her chair out from the kitchen table, stood up and stomped out of the room.

Kelly-Anne wasn't the only one who was in a dark mood at dinner. Stella was clearly in a huff with Issie. As for Aidan, he was barely speaking for some reason and kept glaring at Dan across the table.

"Did you notice that too? He's, like, so totally jealous!" Kate insisted when the girls were gathered in Issie's room later that evening.

"But why?" Issie said. "I've already told him that Dan isn't my boyfriend."

"Maybe," replied Kate, "but it's hard not to notice the way Dan keeps looking at you all the time. And did you see the evils Dan was giving Aidan? He's just as bad!"

"Well, I wish they'd both stop it," Issie sighed. "They can't carry on like this for the next three weeks."

It wasn't just the boys who had Issie worried though. How long could Stella carry on being in a bad mood? Ever since Issie had mentioned her date with Aidan, Stella had been acting really weird. Something was definitely bothering her. She had been really quiet lately. And Stella was never quiet!

Stella would talk to Issie if she needed to, like in the arena when they took the riding lessons. But she wasn't her normal perky, chatty self, and whenever Issie tried to talk to her about what was wrong, she just shrugged and walked away. Issie didn't know what to do. It had seemed like such a good plan for Issie to come here and help Hester. But was she really helping? Right now everything Issie did just seemed to make matters worse.

"Right!" Avery said, eyeing up the riders who were standing in front of him. "I hope you're ready for a workout tonight. We need to get these ponies and horses really fit over the next fortnight – and the best way to do that is lots and lots of circles and flatwork to supple them and get them listening, and then gridwork with the cavaletti so that they develop muscle and rhythm."

Ben looked crushed by the idea of flatwork and cavaletti for two weeks. "But aren't we going to do any big jumps?" he grumbled. "The horses will have to do big jumps in the competition, won't they? Isn't that what we should be practising then?"

Avery nodded. "Absolutely – we'll be doing a few big fences, but not too many. It's important not to overjump these horses. There's too much risk of an injury or making them sour on it. We're going to build up with some smaller courses before the qualifying rounds in a fortnight, and after that we'll start to put the jumps up a notch and tackle some big courses."

Ben didn't look convinced by this argument. You could see he was just itching to take Max around the course of painted rail fences that Avery had set up at the far end of the arena.

"Now, I see you all have your stirrups at jumping length already," Avery smiled. "Very good. But tonight you needn't have bothered."

"You mean we're not jumping at all now?" asked Ben, trying to keep the frustration out of his voice.

Avery shook his head. "No, Ben, you will be jumping – you're just not going to be using your stirrups. We're going to ride without them." He walked over to Ben and quickly slipped both the leathers and irons off his saddle so that Ben had his legs dangling with no stirrups.

"Can you all strip your leathers off the saddle please and hand them over to me?" Avery told the rest of the ride.

"Ohmygod! This feels weird," Stella said as she slipped her stirrups off the saddle and let her legs hang loose down at Coco's sides.

"How are we going to jump without any stirrups?" grumbled Ben.

"You don't need stirrups," Avery insisted. "In fact, relying on your stirrups can teach you bad habits. Learning to jump without them is good for you. It will teach you not to get too far out of the saddle as you go over the fences and you'll be forced to balance and use your knees effectively."

He turned to the riders. "Are we all ready? Let's start work then. Aidan? Can you lead the ride please. Get them working around the arena at a walk and then do a sitting trot in the corner of the arena and come through the cavaletti in your two-point position without stirrups."

There were a few shrieks from Stella and a bit of giggling and bouncing about as the riders got used to trotting without stirrups. But then things got serious as they did the cavaletti course for the first time and they could all see what Avery meant. Without stirrups they were relying on their own body to hold their position and stay in the saddle, and after a few drills back and forth through the cavaletti all of them had a much better seat.

"Excellent," said Avery. "Keep your eyes up, Stella! That's it! Good stuff!" He called all the riders back into the centre of the ring. "Now," he told them with a straight face, "knot your reins please."

Stella couldn't believe this. "You mean we're going to jump with no stirrups and no hands!"

Avery grinned. "Trust me, Stella. It's not as scary as it sounds."

As the horses came bouncing back through the cavaletti at a trot, all the riders managed to stay in the saddle despite having no stirrups and knotted reins. Issie had to hold Comet back as they approached the cavaletti. The skewbald could still get a little fizzy and overexcited when he was taking fences, but as he settled in with the rest of the ride he began to calm down and soon he was trotting the poles like a dream.

"How is he feeling?" Avery asked her as Issie pulled Comet up when they were all getting their stirrups back.

"Really good!" There was a huge smile on Issie's face. "He's a bit hard to hold sometimes though."

"He'll settle down," said Avery. "He's just fresh, that's all." He turned around to the other riders. "That'll do for tonight!" he called out to them. "Good lesson, everyone."

"I can't believe it!" Ben muttered. "When are we going to do some really decent-sized fences?"

It seemed Avery was in no hurry to use the showjumps that were set up at the other end of the arena. For the rest of the week he kept up the same routine, drilling his riders over the cavaletti so that, by the end of it, all of them were quite happy jumping without their stirrups or reins.

The following week, it looked like Ben was finally getting his wish. Avery began to set up a proper jumping course for them to ride. But if the riders had been expecting to jump huge fences, they were disappointed. Avery had built the course with the jumps set low, at a metre high. "We don't need big jumps," he reasoned. "This week is all about learning arena craft. You must be able to ride a showjumping course with technical skill and take the best possible line at a fence. Then, no matter what height you are jumping, your horse will always be in perfect balance."

Comet was a talented jumper, but he wasn't the easiest horse to control. He was inclined to get a little hot and excited when he jumped. "You need to use your seat to control him," Avery told Issie as she took him around the course. "Sit back in the saddle if you want him to slow down. Don't fight him with the reins or he'll just get stroppy with you. Work with him; focus on being a partnership."

Issie worked hard, concentrating on what Avery told her to do, and by the end of the second week she felt like her bond with Comet had strengthened even more.

On Saturday, after the riding school had gone home for the weekend, Avery's riders gathered in the living room of the manor for a squad training meeting.

"The qualifying competition is being held tomorrow," Avery said. "We'll be trucking the horses into the local Gisborne pony-club grounds at 6 a.m. so everyone needs to set their alarm clocks for 5.30 a.m." There was a groan from the riders.

"Meanwhile," Avery continued, "I thought we'd better get the paperwork sorted." He picked up a stack of papers and handed them to Aidan. "You all need to fill in one of these. Can you pass them around please, Aidan?"

"What is it?" Issie asked.

"Your entry form for the Horse of the Year," said Avery.

Issie looked at the entry forms in front of her. Her eyes scanned the long list of competitions and categories.

"I'm thinking of entering Destiny in the Horse of the Year novice category," Aidan said.

Dan, who was also riding hacks now and could no longer enter the pony ring, glared at Aidan. "That's the event that I'm entering on Madonna."

"Then I guess I'll be riding against you," said Aidan gruffly.

"Suits me," Dan bristled.

"What's this one here?" Stella tried to pronounce the word, "The pussy-ance?"

"It's pronounced pwee-sonce," Avery said. "The word 'puissance' is French – it means powerful. It's a high jumping competition basically. The riders jump a brick wall, which gets higher and higher with each round. There are five rounds and it's a knockout competition. If you don't get over the wall, you're out. The idea is to keep jumping until everyone is eliminated. Whoever gets over the highest wall in the last round will be the winner."

"How big can the wall get?" Ben asked.

"The highest a horse has ever jumped in a Puissance competition is two and a half metres."

"Ohmygod!" Stella was amazed. "That's huge!"

Avery stood up and stretched out his arm as far as it would go above his head. "It's about another half a metre taller than my hand," he said.

"I think I saw a Puissance on telly once," Stella said. "The wall was so big you couldn't see the horse at all – all you could see was his ears sticking over the top before he jumped it!"

"How can they jump if they can't even see over it?" Ben boggled.

"The Puissance is all about courage," said Avery. "Once the fence gets to that kind of height, your horse must be truly brave and have faith in his rider because he won't be able to see what's on the other side."

Issie looked back at the entry form and finally found the event she was planning to enter. "This can't be right!" she said. "It says here that the pony Grand Prix has prize money of $15,000! Is that a misprint?"

Avery shook his head. "No. There are over half a million dollars in prizes at this year's Horse of the Year. This is the richest show in the hemisphere. There'll be riders from all around the world competing."

Issie felt her tummy churning with nerves. "Maybe we should enter something else?"

Avery shook his head. "If you qualify, I definitely think it's worth a shot to take on the pony Grand Prix. The jumps are big, but Comet has the ability to do it."

Issie felt her heart racing. "Really? Tom, do you think so?" She looked back at the entry form: $15,000 in prize money! If she won she'd make enough money to help Aunt Hester save Blackthorn Farm!

For a moment, Issie felt so elated at the thought that

she could barely breathe. And then her eyes went to the entry details at the bottom of the form and she felt as if someone had punched her hard in the stomach and knocked the wind clean out of her. There at the bottom of the form was a list of fees. The numbers were quite clearly printed in large black type. Entry fee: $500 per rider, per event.

Five hundred? That was crazy! She didn't have five hundred dollars and she had no way of getting that much money. Her plan was over before she even had a chance – probably her last chance to help her aunt save Blackthorn Farm.

CHAPTER 10

How was Issie going to come up with $500? "There's no point in worrying about that yet," Kate pointed out to her. "We've got to make it through the qualifying rounds before they'll even let us enter Horse of theYear."

The event on Sunday was the last of the district jump-offs. With the finals happening the following weekend, this was the one and only chance for Avery's riders to qualify. The riders were all feeling the pressure as Avery pulled the truck up at the Gisborne Pony Club grounds that morning.

"Only the top ten riders in every event will gain enough points to make it through to the Horse of the Year," Avery told the girls, who were riding in the front with him. "If you don't make it through today's competition then you're out. End of story."

"So there's no pressure then?" Stella said sarcastically. She was busily studying the schedule for the day's events, although Issie suspected that she was mostly reading the schedule as a way of avoiding talking to her. Her long silences during the trip to the club grounds had made it pretty clear that she was still barely speaking to Issie.

"You're lucky!" Kate told Issie when they got out of the truck and began unloading the horses. "It was much worse being in the back with the boys. Dan and Aidan just keep getting at each other all the time! Honestly," she shook her head, "I don't understand boys!"

Things only got worse once the riders saddled up. The running order for the competition was divided into hacks – that's horses fourteen-three hands high and over – and ponies, which are fourteen-two and under. Dan and Aidan were both riding hacks, and that meant that they were riding first.

Both boys were taking the contest really seriously. Their rivalry had been obvious all week at training, but it finally came to a head when they were warming up in the practice arena. There was one jump, a blue and white crossed rail, set up for the riders to practise over before it was their turn in the ring.

The competition was getting hot and Dan was due to ride next. He'd been waiting for his turn and circling Madonna in the practice arena. At the last minute he decided to try one last practice jump and lined up the chestnut mare to take the crossed rails. He didn't seem to notice that Aidan was already riding towards the same jump from the other direction.

"Hey! Get out of my way!" Aidan shouted as he saw Dan riding straight at him. Dan had to put in a last-minute change of direction, yanking at Madonna's head to swerve to get out of Aidan's path.

"Hey, watch it!" he shouted angrily back at Aidan.

"What?" Aidan said. "You're kidding? That was totally your fault! You knew I was going to take the jump. You should have stayed out of my way."

"Well, maybe I'm sick of staying out of your way," Dan shot back at him. He pulled Madonna up to a halt. "I've got to ride now. We'll finish this later," he said coolly.

"Count on it," Aidan replied.

Issie, who was back at the horse truck getting Comet ready, had no idea about any of this. She didn't see the fight at the practice jump and she didn't see Dan and Aidan ride their event. In fact, she would never have found out about what happened next if it hadn't been for Comet's saddle blanket. She had been saddling the skewbald up when she realised she had left her usual blanket behind at the farm.

"Don't worry," Avery had said. "I've got a couple of spare numnahs that should be perfect. They're in the crawlspace above the kitchen."

Horse trucks always have a crawlspace in them – a platform that is built at the top above the living area. Often, when riders go away on long trips in their trucks to compete, they will sleep on a mattress in the crawlspace. Avery had been planning to sleep there himself on this trip, but since they'd had a change of plans and he was now staying at the manor, he'd shoved all sorts of things into the empty space – including spare saddle blankets.

Issie had climbed up the ladder to the crawlspace and was lying on her belly, feeling around in the half-light for the saddle blankets, when she heard the stomp of footsteps in the living space underneath her. She could hear two voices quite clearly and she recognised them immediately. It was Dan and Aidan, and if they sounded mad with each other before, now they were furious.

"You could have lost me the competition today with that stunt over the practice fence," Dan fumed.

"Me?" Aidan was flabbergasted. "Dude! You cut me off. And you did it on purpose!"

Dan snorted. "That's ridiculous. Why would I do that?"

"You know why," Aidan said. "Because Issie chose me and you can't stand it."

Dan glowered at him. "You're dreaming, man. I don't know where you get the idea from that you're her boyfriend, but you're wrong."

"Why don't you just back off and leave me and Issie alone?" Aidan said, his face dark and brooding under his black fringe.

"I was about to say the same thing," said Dan. Then he looked Aidan square in the eyes. "Listen, it's time to settle this, right? So how about we do it in the arena?"

"What do you mean?"

"The Horse of the Year," Dan said. "We've both qualified to ride in it, right? So what about if we make a little bet?"

"What sort of bet?"

"I should have thought that was obvious," Dan replied.

Aidan looked at him. "You mean bet on who gets Issie?"

"Uh-huh," Dan said. "Whoever wins the competition gets to be her boyfriend."

Aidan looked at him. "So if I win, you'll back off and leave me and her alone?"

"Yeah," Dan said. "If you win. Which you won't."

Aidan bit his lip, then he shook his head. "This is stupid. Issie will never agree to it anyway."

"Then we won't tell her," said Dan. "This is just between you and me." He put out his hand. "Or are you too scared to take me on?"

Aidan looked Dan in the eye. And then he took his hand and shook it hard. "You've got a bet."

Upstairs, in the crawlspace of the truck, Issie felt herself trembling. She was shaking partly out of fear – she would have hated to have been discovered right now – but mostly out of pure anger. How dare those boys bargain with her as if she were a Bella Sara card to be traded? They were totally crazy! She held her breath and lay perfectly still in the crawlspace for another minute or so and then slowly stuck her head out to make sure they were gone. There was no one there.

As she backed out down the ladder her heart was still

beating like mad. She couldn't believe what she had just heard! At moments like these, Issie realised, there was only one person in the world that she could talk to about stuff like this. She needed her best friend right now. Unfortunately, Stella wasn't speaking to her.

Issie looked at her watch. She was due at the arena to compete in ten minutes. That didn't leave her much time. But she knew she had no choice. Stella was her best friend. How could things have got so messed up? She needed to talk to her desperately and straighten things out. Issie couldn't possibly concentrate on the competition and riding her horse until she had made things right with her best friend.

Luckily for Issie, Stella wasn't too hard to find. Her red curly hair was easy to spot across the fields. Issie could see her by the main arena, leaning over the railings by herself and watching the last of the hacks compete in the open classes.

As Issie approached Stella she thought of everything she wanted to say. She wanted to say that she never meant to make Stella feel left out. She wanted to let Stella know that she was her best friend in the world and that she would never let a boy come between them. She wanted to tell Stella that they were best friends forever and it was a silly fight and she missed her. But, in fact, when she arrived at Stella's side with tears shining in her eyes, all she said was, "I'm sorry!" and that was enough. Before Issie knew it, Stella had said she was sorry too and the two friends were hugging and giggling and saying, "Let's pretend it never happened, OK?" And Issie was telling Stella the whole story of the contest between Dan and Aidan and they were pulling faces over how crazy boys were and then laughing so hard they were gasping for air.

"Ohmygod!" Stella said. "This is like the best thing ever! They've made a bet and the winner gets to be your boyfriend? What planet are they on?"

Issie shook her head. "It's like they're medieval knights in a jousting match and I'm the fair maiden."

"Well, fair maiden." Stella did a little bow and a curtsey. "Who dost thou think will win your hand?"

"I don't know," Issie said.

"Well, it doesn't matter who wins, does it?" Stella said. "They don't get to decide who gets you. You should be the one who gets to choose."

"Stella, that's just the problem," Issie looked serious. "I guess I've been trying for ages. You know, to choose between Aidan and Dan…"

"And?"

Issie sighed. "I don't know. I can't decide."

"Well, if you want to know who I'd choose…" Stella was about to offer her opinion when Issie froze and looked at the arena.

"The open hack event has finished!" she said. She checked her watch. "Ohmygod! The pony Grand Prix qualifier is next and I haven't even got Comet saddled up!"

"Come on," Stella said, breaking into a run beside Issie. "Let's get back to the truck. I can saddle Comet while you get changed. It's OK, we'll make it in time."

"Isadora! Where have you been? You're due at the practice arena now!" Avery was far from pleased as Stella and Issie came running towards the horse truck.

"Sorry, Tom," Issie said. "I lost track of the time."

"It was my fault really," Stella added. "Issie came to find me and I made her late."

Avery looked at them both and shook his head. "I have no idea what the pair of you have been up to, but lucky for you I've already saddled Comet up." He tossed Issie her helmet. "Put this on and grab your boots. Let's go."

As Avery gave her a leg-up on to Comet's back, he offered Issie some last-minute advice. "This is a qualifying competition. There's no clock to beat; all you have to worry about is jumping cleanly. Get a clear round and you'll be guaranteed a place in the Horse of the Year."

Avery tightened Issie's girth by a hole and checked her stirrup length. "Now, you've walked the course twice already this morning. Do you know which route you're taking?" Issie nodded.

"OK, then give him a brisk trot around to warm him up, and pop him over the practice rails a couple of times before you go into the arena." He gave Comet's gear a final check, "You're all set. Any questions?"

Issie shook her head. Any questions she had about whether she was ready for this, about whether Comet was truly ready, would be answered in just a moment when they rode into the ring.

As Issie warmed her horse up around the practice ring, she took the same approach with Comet that she had done right from the start. The skewbald was so headstrong that he liked to do things his own way. *Well, fine*, Issie thought, *let him run the show. Let Comet set his own pace and find his own stride between the fences. Interfere with him as little as possible and never, ever fight him. Just stay one step ahead of him, anticipate, be ready to react.*

As Comet danced about in front of the practice jump, it was as if he expected Issie to take a firm hold on his reins and pull him back. But she didn't. Instead, she gave the pony his head and stayed perfectly calm. She focused her energy on keeping him steady and straight, letting the pony relax as he approached the jump, as if the cross-rails weren't even there and she didn't care. Once Comet had taken the practice jump and understood that Issie wasn't going to try and control him or yank on his mouth, he calmed down too. Now Issie gathered Comet up, holding him just a little with the reins so that he rounded his neck and brought his hocks under him. She looked over at Avery, who was standing on the sideline with Stella. Avery nodded back to her as if to say, "That's it, you've got him ready to go."

Issie nodded back and, at the sound of her name being called, she entered the arena. There weren't many people here at the qualifying rounds today, but even a very small audience was good enough for Comet. As he came through the flags and took the first jump he gave a dramatic tail flick. Over the first fence he kicked his hind legs out with a baroque flourish, putting much more air between him and the jump than he actually needed to. Then he approached the second fence and took that with the same outlandish jumping style.

"He jumps like a circus pony," Stella giggled.

"Yes," agreed Avery, "but look how cleanly he always takes a fence. The way he kicks his hind feet up like that so that they never so much as scrape a rail. I've spent years training my showjumpers to take fences so cleanly. Comet does it naturally."

Out in the arena, Issie felt her adrenalin surge as Comet cleared fence after fence with ease. Issie tried to stay calm, to keep a firm but light hold on the reins, controlling her pony simply by sitting up in the saddle if she wanted him to slow down, letting Comet control the pace. As they rounded the corner to set up the final combination in the course, a double with a bounce stride in the middle of it, Issie felt that Comet was cantering a little too fast, and for the first time on the course, she checked him with a sharp signal on the reins. She knew it was risky. Comet might overreact, fight her pressure and go even faster. But the skewbald didn't argue with her at all. He slowed his stride just as she had requested, and then took off perfectly over the first fence, bouncing in and popping back out over the second with that trademark flourish of his hind legs. Issie felt a thrill tingle through her. Not because they had just got a clear round and made it through to the Horse of the Year Show. Something much more important had just happened in the arena; Issie and Comet had experienced that breakthrough moment. When she asked Comet to slow down and he took her cues without a fight, both horse and rider knew that they were truly working together. It was a partnership. And if they could maintain that partnership, they would be unbeatable.

CHAPTER 11

Issie pressed her ear up against the receiver and listened to the ring tone. She could hear the phone ringing once, twice, three times... Please, please pick up! She was just about to hang up again when finally the receiver clicked and there was a familiar voice at the other end of the line.

"Hello? This is Amanda Brown speaking."

"Mum?" Issie croaked. "It's me."

"Issie?" Her mother sounded concerned. "It's nearly eleven o'clock at night. Are you OK?"

"I'm fine, Mum. Are Blaze and Storm OK?"

"They're fine, Issie. I checked them this afternoon. Is that why you called?"

"No..."

"Issie, is there something wrong?"

"I'm fine, it's just… ummm… Mum? Can I borrow $500?"

There was silence on the other end of the phone for a moment and then Mrs Brown's gentle voice. "OK, Issie, why don't you start at the beginning and tell me just what's going on."

Half an hour later Issie had told her mother everything. She told her all about the farm being in trouble and Comet, and how she'd been training him to win the pony Grand Prix and had already made it through the qualifying rounds.

"…And the prize money is $15,000! It's almost enough to save the farm!" Issie said. There was silence at the other end of the phone. "So… umm what do you think?"

"I think that $500 is a lot of money," Mrs Brown replied matter-of-factly.

"I know it is, Mum, but I really think Comet can do this," said Issie. "I'll pay you back. I have some savings from when I did *The Palomino Princess* and I was going to use that money to buy Blaze a new winter rug, but you can have that and…"

"All right," Mrs Brown said quietly.

"What?" Issie was stunned.

"I said all right. Yes, I'll lend you the $500." There was silence on the phone line. "Issie? Are you still there?"

"Uh-huh. I just can't believe you said yes."

"Neither can I," Mrs Brown said. "Now I'm going to give you my credit card number to put on the entry form and if I were you I'd shut up and write it down before I change my mind about the whole thing."

After she hung up the phone, Issie went upstairs to her bedroom. She propped up the envelope containing her entry on the mantelpiece underneath the portrait of Avignon. Then she lay down on her four-poster bed and stared up at the ceiling. She was in a state of shock. Was she really going to do this? She was entered in the biggest competition of her whole life on a horse that was green as grass and she had just asked her mum to give her $500 to do it!

It wasn't that Issie was having second thoughts, or an attack of nerves. No. What she was feeling now was pure adrenalin and excitement at the thought of taking Comet into the show ring and proving to everyone what an amazing horse he really was. She knew the heart and the courage that Comet had; there was no doubt in her mind that he could do it. It was up to Issie now. If she could ride her best, if she did everything right and didn't make any mistakes then they could totally ace this.

With only a week to go until the competition, she needed to get really serious about training. The Horse of the Year was next Sunday and this week was going to be the most testing time of her life.

"Issie! Issie! George keeps poking his tongue out at me! Make him stop!"

Issie sighed. She had been expecting this week to be gruelling, but she hadn't figured on this! Not only did she have a heavy training schedule, but she still had her riding-school duties to contend with as well. That included keeping George in line when he tried to tease his sister.

"I wasn't doing anything!" George objected when Issie told him to stop pestering Kitty.

"George, please circle Glennie through the arena so that you are at the rear of the ride," Issie instructed. "If you two can't behave when you're riding next to each other then it's better if you stay at the back. Kitty? Can you get Timmy trotting a bit more rhythmically please?

He's moving like a slug at the moment. Put your leg on and get him striding out. One-two, one-two! Excellent! Much better!"

For the past week, Issie, Stella and Kate had been leading a double life, training the young riders during the day, grooming and cleaning the stables and feeding the kids their dinner before saddling up their own horses and riding their evening training sessions with Avery.

"I feel ready to drop," Stella complained as the girls lay on Issie's bed that evening. "Those kids are a total nightmare. George is out of control and Kelly-Anne has such a bad attitude."

"Well," Issie said, forcing herself to stand up again, "forget about them for now. It's time to get down to the stables and get ready for team training."

Stella groaned and didn't move. "I don't know why I'm even bothering with training. I'm not even riding in the stupid Horse of the Year." Coco and Stella had managed two very good rounds at the qualifying competition – unfortunately, neither of them were good enough.

"I only got twelve faults," Stella whined. "Can you believe that wasn't enough to qualify?"

"How do you think I feel?" Kate said. Toby, Kate's

rangy bay Thoroughbred, was a well-schooled jumper, but when they got to the showgrounds on the day he had trotted up lame. Avery thought it was probably just a stone bruise. There was a farrier working at the showgrounds who had come straightaway and replaced the shoe, but Kate hadn't been convinced that Toby was one hundred per cent so she decided not to compete.

"He doesn't seem to be lame now though, that's the main thing," Kate said, trying hard to be cheerful about it. "Hopefully he's totally sound again and we can do the training for the rest of the week."

As Avery had promised, the fences had got bigger this week. The riders had been doing substantial showjumping courses, working on getting their striding correct between jumps and learning how to hold their horses back between fences.

The showjumping course had grown too. Avery had packed his horse truck with his own equipment from Winterflood Farm. One of the new jumps that he had built was a wall constructed out of red painted "bricks" that were made from lightweight wood. Avery had even added the finishing touches by putting a tall conifer plant at either corner of the wall.

On Thursday night Avery lined up the riders in front

of the brick wall and they watched as he added in an extra row of bricks to make it higher.

"Now, I know none of you are actually entered in the Puissance this weekend," Avery said, "but we're going to practise it anyway. It's a good way to find out what your horse's limits are, just how high they can really jump."

"So how does it work?" asked Stella. "We just take turns jumping the wall until someone has a refusal or knocks down a brick and then they're out?"

"That's pretty much it," Avery said. "There are actually two fences in the Puissance. You have to jump a basic painted rail fence before you turn to take the wall. The painted rail will stay at the same height for the whole of the competition. Only the wall gets bigger each time. And actually, you are allowed a refusal. You'll only be eliminated if your horse refuses three times, or if you knock a brick or choose to withdraw because the jump gets too high."

Avery looked back at the wall. "I've set it at a metre ten to begin with. There's a maximum of five rounds in a Puissance, so tonight we'll be raising the height by ten centimetres each time. We should finish at a metre fifty – if anyone makes it that far. OK," he said, "who wants to go first?"

"I will!" Aidan and Dan both answered at once. The boys glared at each other.

"Aidan, you can go first," Avery decided before they could start squabbling. "The rest of you, start warming your horses up."

The first round, unsurprisingly, saw all six riders go clear. "Too easy!" Ben called out as he cantered back to Avery after clearing the wall without any trouble on Max. He was eating his words a few minutes later when Max knocked a brick out in the second round.

In round three, Kate withdrew on Toby, who seemed to be having a problem again with the same leg that had gone lame the other day. "He's probably fine and I'm just being a fusspot," Kate said to Avery, "but I don't want to jump him too high if he is a bit sore."

That left Stella, Issie, Aidan and Dan still in the competition. The wall had been raised to a metre forty for the fourth round. On the sidelines the Blackthorn Riders were all cheering and shouting.

"Boys against girls! Boys win!" called a voice from the arena railing. Issie turned around to see Arthur's cheeky face staring up at her.

"Don't count on it, Arthur!" she shouted back.

There was whooping from the girls on the sidelines

as Stella turned to face the wall at one metre forty – and then cries of dismay as Coco refused and Stella flew forward on to the mare's neck and had to struggle to stay on. She turned her pony away from the wall and trotted her back over to Avery. "I think that's Coco's limit," she said. "That's way the highest we've ever jumped in our whole lives!"

Avery nodded. "I agree. Good decision to stop her there, Stella – and a great jumping effort."

The boys on the sidelines had their second disappointment when Dan attempted the metre forty wall and Madonna dropped her feet and knocked out a brick.

"Bad luck," said Issie as he rode off. Then she pushed Comet into a canter and began to prepare to take the wall for the fourth time. Comet popped easily over the painted rails – and even more easily over the metre forty wall, giving his usual heel flick and clearing the top of the fence with room to spare!

The girls on the sideline went wild – except for Kelly-Anne, who was creeping Issie out by sitting on the railing all by herself and staring at Comet with greedy eyes.

Issie was the only one to make the height of a metre forty so far. That just left Aidan to try his luck. "Get ready for a jump-off," he grinned at Issie as he breezed past her at a canter to face the warm-up fence.

But there wasn't going to be a jump-off at all. Destiny did exactly the same thing that Madonna had done, dropping his hind legs just enough to dislodge a brick and dashing his chances to the ground.

"Issie wins on round four!" Avery announced.

There was much bragging from the girls on the sideline and Kitty was pulling faces at George. "Girls rule!"

Avery walked over to Issie with a broad grin on his face. "That was very nicely taken at a metre forty," he said.

Issie beamed. "Comet took it easily."

"He's got an amazing jump in him," Avery said, "and a very clean pair of hind feet." Then he added cryptically, "It'd be interesting to see just how high he could go."

The next day, the girls decided that since the kids had enjoyed watching the Puissance so much, they would have one of their own for the riding-school pupils.

"Cool!" George yelled. "A chance for the boys to win their glory back!"

Stella rolled her eyes, and Kitty looked nervous.

"We're not going over the big wall like last night, are we?"

"We're going to use the wall," Stella said, "but we'll make it much lower. We're going to start it at twenty centimetres."

The riders were all lining up ready to go when Kelly-Anne rode forward on Julian with a face as sour as month-old milk. "I don't think it's fair," she said, fixing Issie with a determined look. "Julian is a useless jumper so there's no way I'll win."

"Kelly-Anne," Issie said through gritted teeth, "we've been through this a million times. Julian is actually quite a good showjumper and he's perfectly capable of doing jumps like this."

Kelly-Anne sneered. "I was watching you last night. You think you're a really good rider, but you're not. It's just because you have a good horse. That's why you won't let me ride Comet, isn't it? I bet I could ride him just as well as you can! Go and saddle him up for me! I want to ride Comet!"

For weeks now Kelly-Anne had been the riding school's resident pain in the neck. She was rude to the other riders, mean to the horses and grumpy to her instructors, but this was the worst, most miserable outburst yet. Issie didn't know what to say. But luckily, as it turned out, she didn't need to say anything because Aunty Hess was standing behind the riders and had heard everything.

"That's it, Kelly-Anne!" Hester barked. "You've had plenty of warnings. That's the final straw. You should never speak to a riding instructor like that."

Kelly-Anne stuck her bottom lip out. "But I wasn't doing anything. I was just saying…"

"I heard everything you said, Kelly-Anne." Hester's voice was firm but calm. "You can take Julian back to the stables please. Stella will come and help you unsaddle him. I'm not willing to put up with this behaviour in my school any longer. I'm calling your mother, and you can pack your bags. You're going home."

Kelly-Anne was too stunned for once to bite back. She looked like she was trying very hard not to cry as she turned Julian around and headed back to the stables. The rest of the riders sat there on their ponies watching her leave.

"Serves her right!" George muttered.

"George!" Issie told him off. She had never thought she would feel sorry for a girl like Kelly-Anne, but at that moment, as she watched her riding back to the stables alone, she felt sympathy for Kelly-Anne for the first time.

Kelly-Anne didn't turn up for dinner that night.

"She's probably embarrassed," Hester said. "Let's leave her alone. I've spoken to her mother, and she wasn't at all surprised. Apparently she's been having some trouble at home. Her parents are going through a rather nasty divorce – which I didn't realise. Anyway, they sent her away to pony camp to keep her out of the firing line, so her mother wasn't exactly pleased to hear she needed to come and pick her up. She's coming to get her tomorrow after breakfast."

The punishment of being sent home was doubly cruel, Issie now realised. If Kelly-Anne's mum came to get her on Saturday, she wouldn't be able to come with the other riders to the Horse of the Year Show on the Sunday as they'd planned.

"It's her own fault," Stella said when Issie pointed this out. Still, Issie couldn't help but feel bad about being responsible for getting Kelly-Anne sent home. She knew how awful she had felt when her parents split up. Maybe she had misjudged Kelly-Anne a little.

Issie was exhausted by the time she went to bed that night. She had big plans to read her manual of showjumping rules to make sure she was ready for Sunday, but the boring rule book made her eyelids immediately feel heavy and she gave up and switched out the light.

It was just before dawn when she was woken up by a sound outside her bedroom. Issie sat bolt upright in bed. She could have sworn she had heard hoofbeats outside – and her first thought was that Comet had jumped the fence again. Then she realised that she had left him in his loose box last night. It couldn't be Comet. Maybe she was imagining it? She slid out of bed and felt the cool wood of the floorboards against her bare feet as she tiptoed over to the window.

The sunlight was beginning to creep across the horizon. Issie guessed that it must have been about 6 a.m. In the early morning gloom, she could make out shapes and shadows on the lawn down below her bedroom. As she was standing there, with her nose pressed against the glass, she realised that one of these shadows, right in the middle of the lawn, was moving.

Issie stayed perfectly still. Was the shadow really moving or was she imagining it? There was no doubt in her mind a few moments later when the light picked out the colours of the shadow-shape and she saw a flash of dapple-grey, the shimmer of silver mane. The shadow on the lawn below was her horse. It was Mystic!

Issie pulled on a pair of jeans, not bothering to change out of her pyjama top, and hurried down the stairs. At the back door she shoved on her riding boots before racing across the lawn to the place where she had seen Mystic.

The horse wasn't there any more, but as she looked around, Issie thought she caught a glimpse of him again, heading between the trees towards the stables. Issie could hardly breathe. It was like her heart was in her throat, choking all the air out of her as she ran across the back lawn. By the time she reached the stables, she was gasping for air and had to bend over for a moment with her hands on her knees to catch her breath. She stood up again and looked around, expecting to see Mystic, but the grey gelding wasn't there. Had he been there at all or had she just imagined it? No, Issie had been quite sure it was Mystic on the lawn, but why was he here now?

Panic gripped her as a thought occurred. The last time Mystic was here he had been watching over Comet. Was that why the grey gelding was here? She looked down the row of loose boxes to the stall at the far end. It was still bolted shut, just as she had left it when she put Comet in herself last night.

"Comet?" she yelled out as she began to run up the row to the stall. "It's OK, boy, I'm here." Issie fell against the door of the stall and struggled to work the top bolt free to swing it open. Inside the stall, Comet didn't respond. The awful silence from behind the door gave Issie a chill of fear. Her fingers fumbled desperately as she opened the stall.

"Comet?" she said softly. She was still hoping that the pony would appear and thrust his cute little skewbald face out to greet her. But the minute she opened the top door she could see that this wasn't going to happen. She braced herself and stuck her head over, expecting to see the worst. But she wasn't prepared for what she actually saw. Her pony wasn't in his stall at all. The loose box was totally empty. Comet was gone.

CHAPTER 12

Stay calm! Issie told herself. Comet couldn't just disappear. That was crazy. She must be confused. Maybe she put him back in a different stall last night? Or perhaps Hester or Aidan had changed their minds and put him out to graze instead? No! She knew where she had put him last night – the stall she was standing in right now. She hadn't moved him and neither had anyone else. He had simply disappeared.

Issie took a deep breath. Horses didn't just disappear. She had to calm down and think clearly to make sense of this.

Acting on a hunch, she ran out of Comet's stall, sprinting all the way down the stable corridor to the tack room. Her blood pounding and heart racing, she grabbed the tack-room key from its hiding place on a nail behind the hat on the wall and fumbled to work the padlock. The lock was fiddly and her hands were trembling. It finally came open and Issie barged straight through the door and into the dark room on the other side.

She switched on the tack-room light and began frantically scanning the racks of saddles and bridles. She soon found what she was looking for – or rather she didn't find it. Comet's saddle and bridle were both missing.

Well, that solved part of the mystery. Comet hadn't disappeared by himself. Someone had taken him. But who would do that? There was the shuffle of footsteps behind her and Issie turned to see Kitty in her pyjamas looking pale and scared beneath the stable lights.

"Ohmygod, Kitty!" Issie gasped. "Don't sneak up like that! You startled me! What are you doing here?"

"Kelly-Anne took him," Kitty said.

"What?"

"Kelly-Anne. She took Comet. She woke me up. I was asleep and I heard a noise and then I saw her dressed in her jodhpurs so I asked her where she was going. She said it was unfair, that she wanted to ride Comet but you would never let her. She wanted to ride him just once before her mum came to take her home. I told her she shouldn't do it, but she got really angry at me and made me promise not to tell anyone…"

Kitty looked like she was going to cry. "I'm really sorry, Issie. I should have tried to stop her. It's all my fault…"

Issie shook her head. "You did the right thing, telling me. And don't worry about Kelly-Anne. I'll find her and I'll get Comet back and everything will be OK, I promise." Kitty wiped her nose with the sleeve of her pyjamas.

"How long ago did she leave?" Issie asked her.

"Ages ago," Kitty said, sniffling. "She said she'd be back again by breakfast and no one would ever know she had taken him."

"OK, Kitty, I need you to do something else for me," Issie said. "Can you go and find Aunty Hess and tell her that Kelly-Anne has taken Comet and I've gone to follow her? Can you do that for me?"

Kitty nodded and then she turned and set off down the long corridor past the stalls and out the back of the stables, heading for the manor, leaving Issie standing alone in the tack room.

Issie's mind flashed back to that jumping lesson when Kelly-Anne had lost her temper with Julian. She still remembered Julian's wild eyes, the poor pony's terror and confusion as Kelly-Anne had whipped him again and again in front of the jump.

If she does anything like that to Comet, if she hurts my horse... Issie was almost shaking with anger. What did Kelly-Anne think she was doing? Comet was too fiery for her to handle. Kelly-Anne simply didn't listen and now she was going to get herself hurt – and Comet too!

Issie looked back at the racks of bridles and saddles. Kelly-Anne had a head start. She would need a fast horse if she wanted to catch up with her. Her first thought was Destiny. The black horse had a huge stride, plus he had grown up on the hills around the farm and he was sure-footed across country. But then she remembered that Aidan was planning to ride the stallion in the Horse of the Year. Taking Destiny on a ride like this the day before the event was crazy. The farm terrain was uneven and rough and there was every chance that Destiny might stand in a rabbit hole or throw a shoe. If he went lame then Aidan would be devastated and Issie would never forgive herself. No, she couldn't risk it.

Her next choice was Diablo. The piebald was fit

and almost as fast at a gallop as Destiny. She grabbed Diablo's saddle and bridle from the rack and ran down the corridor to his stall. The black and white Quarter Horse gave a nicker of surprise as she opened the door to his loose box and stepped inside.

"Hey, Diablo," Issie said. "We're in a hurry so no grooming today, OK, boy?"

She threw the saddle straight on to the piebald's back and did up the girth. Then she adjusted the stirrups to a short length. She was going to be riding fast and for the sake of speed she would need to stay up in two-point position in the saddle the whole time.

As she slipped on Diablo's bridle and did up the throat lash, Issie heard noises out in the corridor. "Kitty?" she called out. "Are you still here? I thought I told you to go up to the house?"

But when she led Diablo out of his stall there was no one there. Issie looked back down the row of stalls. They were all shut tight apart from Comet and Diablo's boxes. The place was empty. She turned again to lead Diablo out the back of the stables through the open doors towards the paddocks and that was when she saw him.

Standing in the doorway, framed by the dawn light,

was a grey pony. Issie could see the soft bloom of his dappled coat and the thick silvery mane shining, his coal black eyes staring intently at her.

"Mystic!" she called out. The grey gelding raised his head and nickered to her, and Issie waited, expecting her pony to come to her as he always did. But he didn't come closer; he shifted about restlessly, dancing this way and that, shaking his mane in agitation.

"Mystic?" Something was wrong. Issie dropped Diablo's reins and began to run towards him, but it was too late. Mystic had already turned on his hocks and set off at a canter, disappearing through the stable doors and out of sight.

"Mystic!" Issie began to run faster, her blood pounding, pulse racing. Why didn't her pony wait for her? When she reached the stable doors and ran outside she almost expected him to be gone, and was a little surprised to see him standing waiting for her next to the paddocks beyond the cottage. "Mystic!" she called out. The grey gelding didn't move. Issie didn't understand. Mystic had never been like this before. Why wouldn't he come to her? Then the thought occurred to her. *He wants me to follow him!*

Well, she realised, she wouldn't get far like this.

She needed Diablo. When Issie had dropped Diablo's reins to run off after Mystic, the Quarter Horse had remembered his stunt training and stayed rooted to the spot where Issie had left him at the far end of the stables.

Issie spun around to face him, put her fingers to her lips and blew a short, sharp whistle. Diablo reacted to this cue as if on pure instinct. Without hesitation, he broke into a canter, his hooves clattering on the concrete floor of the stables as he ran to Issie's side.

"Good boy, Diablo," Issie said, grabbing the reins and swinging herself swiftly on to the stunt horse's back. "Let's go."

Mystic was still standing by the paddocks waiting for them, but the moment he saw Issie and Diablo emerge from the stables he turned away and began to canter ahead of them, towards the back fence of the paddock and the rise of Blackthorn Hill. The countryside beyond the fenceline was hilly and the terrain was rough and covered with scrub. There was no path or clear ground to ride over. Issie would never have come this way herself. She would have ridden along the well-worn ridge track. But she quickly understood why Mystic was leading her this way. It may be more dangerous, but it would take half the time.

Issie clucked Diablo into a canter and they began

gaining on Mystic, who was heading straight for the back fence. Issie scanned the fenceline, looking for the gate. She didn't realise the flaw in Mystic's plan until it was too late. There was no gate. If they were going to get to the other side, they were going to have to jump their way out.

Issie looked at the fence. It was a post and rails, about one metre twenty. Comet would clear a fence like that easily. But could Mystic and Diablo? As the grey gelding approached the fence, Issie held her breath. She needn't have worried. Mystic took the fence with ease, his legs forming a graceful arc above the rails. He looked just like a dolphin diving, Issie realised. A perfect bascule!

She was getting close to the fence herself now and, considering she had never even seen the piebald jump a fence before, let alone ridden him over one herself, she decided she would just have to ride hard at it. As Diablo approached the back fence she heard him give a nervous snort, as if he had only just realised what she was asking him to do.

"You can do it, Diablo!" Issie said, putting all her faith into the horse, willing him to take the jump. Diablo sensed her confidence and, as he came into the fence he didn't hesitate; his stride stayed steady as he took off and flew over the rails, landing cleanly on the other side without breaking stride. "Good boy!" Issie gave him a firm pat on his black and white patchy neck, her eyes remaining on Mystic, who was now galloping on ahead of them, across the rough gorse and scrub towards the crest of Blackthorn Hill.

As they galloped on and up the hill Issie caught a glimpse of some cross-country jumps to her left and remembered what Aidan had said about building a course across the farm. As she rode over the crest of Blackthorn Hill and looked down on the valley she could see several cross-country obstacles scattered over the paddocks below. To her left now she could also see the winding red snake of dirt that was the ridge track. Her cross-country route must have saved her at least twenty minutes, maybe more. Had she caught up with Kelly-Anne and Comet? Maybe she had even overtaken them? She looked up and down the track. Where were they?

There was a whinny from Mystic, who was already barrelling back down the other side of Blackthorn Hill, ducking and swerving his way around blackthorns and gorse as he headed helter-skelter at a gallop towards the valley below. Issie's eyes followed the grey gelding, and then her heart leapt as she caught sight of another horse ahead of Mystic in the distance. It was Comet! The skewbald was about half a kilometre ahead. She could see him clearly next to one of Aidan's jumps.

"Come on, Diablo." Issie clucked the horse into a gallop, through the scrub and the long grass, following Mystic down the sheer face of the hill.

If you have ever galloped downhill, you will know that it's terrifying. It would have been hard enough for Issie galloping downhill on the ridge track, but here on the uneven ground of Blackthorn Hill, with Diablo dodging this way and that to avoid the prickly gorse and blackthorn bushes, it was a total nightmare. All Issie could do was hold on and stick to the path that Mystic had taken ahead of her, trusting in the grey gelding to show them the safest way to go. Issie bit her lip to hold back her fear. She wanted to tell the little grey pony to slow down, but as they drew nearer she became even more afraid of what lay ahead.

Kelly-Anne had obviously tried to take Comet over one of Aidan's cross-country jumps, a stacked logpile, and something must have gone wrong. Very wrong. Comet was standing stock-still and Kelly-Anne was no longer on his back. Issie could see her body lying sprawled and motionless on the ground next to the jump, with Comet standing over her. Comet raised his head a little when he caught sight of Diablo and Mystic, but other than that, the skewbald didn't move a muscle. He was standing next to the girl, still as a statue! But Comet never stood still. He was always dancing about. Something was definitely wrong!

As they came into closer range Issie could finally see why her pony wasn't moving. Instinctively, she pressed Diablo on to gallop even harder. She couldn't afford to slow down; she had to reach her horse before things got any worse. Comet wasn't standing next to the logpile, he was standing in the logpile. His front leg had somehow got wedged between two rails of the rustic fence. He was standing perfectly still because he had no choice. If he moved or tried to pull his leg free, the pony would rip the skin from his cannon bone or even break a leg as he tried to wrench his hoof out.

At the sight of Issie and Mystic, the skewbald gave a frantic whinny and began to try and free himself.

"Comet! No!" Issie called out. He had to stay still until she could reach him. She urged Diablo on faster now. She had to get to Comet.

Please, please don't move, she thought. *Stay still just a little bit longer, Comet. I'm coming…*

CHAPTER 13

As she pulled Diablo up next to the logpile, Issie wanted more than anything to rush to Comet's side, but first she needed to see if Kelly-Anne was OK. Issie vaulted off Diablo's back, running over to the girl, who lay motionless on the ground.

"Kelly-Anne?" Issie put her hand on her shoulder and shook her gently. She didn't move. She must have been knocked out cold from the fall. Quickly, Issie tried to remember what they had taught her in the first-aid sessions at pony club. *Don't move her, and check her breathing.* She looked at her chest and could see it rising and falling. Good. Kelly-Anne was definitely breathing.

"Kelly-Anne, can you hear me?" Issie tried again. This time there was a groan and the girl murmured, her eyelids fluttering. She was waking up.

"What happened?" Kelly-Anne said groggily.

"You've had an accident," said Issie. "Don't try to move yet. Just lie still. I'll be back in a moment."

Now she was certain that Kelly-Anne was OK she was finally able to get a closer look at Comet. The skewbald had been standing still all this time, waiting patiently for Issie to come to him.

"Hey, Comet," Issie said. "It's going to be OK, boy."

At first glance, though, Issie wasn't sure things were going to be OK at all. Comet was shivering with shock. His flanks were damp with sweat and he was covered in mud. But what really worried Issie was Comet's leg. The pony's near foreleg was completely wedged through the shattered wood rails of the logpile fence. By the look of the angle, he had brought the leg down on top of the jump and his hoof had rammed straight through the wood. The weathered timber had splintered under the sheer force of the pony's hoof so that Comet was now stuck knee-deep in the logpile. Luckily, Comet had had the common sense to recognise his predicament and had stood still, waiting for his rider to free him. Only Kelly-Anne was in no fit state to help him at all.

How long had Comet been standing there like this? Issie wondered. And what would have happened if she hadn't arrived in time? Even now that Issie was here to help him, the skewbald was still in a perilous position. He was terrified. Issie could see the whites of his eyes and knew the pony was exhausted with stress and fear. How long would it be before he lost his cool and went into a frenzy, trying to free himself at any cost? Issie felt the panic rising in her too; she knew she had to act fast.

"Easy, boy," she cooed as she moved slowly towards Comet. She had to be careful. A sudden movement might spook him and if he pulled back he would wrench his leg horribly against the pointy barbs of broken wood.

"Easy, Comet," she said. "It's OK, boy," she whispered as she stroked the skewbald's neck. "Steady, boy, that's a good Comet, steady…" Her hands ran along his neck and down his near foreleg, the one that was wedged tight into the logpile. "Easy, Comet," Issie soothed him, stroking his neck and looking at the leg. "Stay still. I'll get you out, I promise. There's a good boy…"

"He's not a good boy, he's a stupid, mean pony!" It was Kelly-Anne. She was on her knees and looking dazed and wobbly as she struggled to clamber back up on to her feet.

"Kelly-Anne!" Issie said. "Don't get up. You've had a bad fall and you were knocked out. Sit down for a minute and catch your breath." For once, Kelly-Anne seemed to listen. She collapsed back against the logpile.

"No!" Issie said. "Not on the rails! You'll crush his leg if you sit there! Get off!"

Kelly-Anne staggered back up and looked at Comet. "It's his own fault," she said. "He wouldn't jump it. I was trying to jump the logpile and he wouldn't go over and then he stopped in front of it so I whacked him and he still wouldn't go over so I hit him again and then he did this stupid sort of bunny hop and I guess he must have landed on top of the fence and that was when I fell off…"

Issie felt her blood boil. She knew it! It was exactly the same back at the riding school when Kelly-Anne had terrified poor Julian.

"I don't want to hear any more!" Issie snapped. "It's always the horse's fault, isn't it? Well, I've got news for you, Kelly-Anne. It's your fault. You're a nightmare. You shouldn't even be allowed to ride. You don't know anything about horses and, even worse, you don't seem to care about them either!"

All the blood drained from Kelly-Anne's face as Issie said this. The girl stood there for a moment, too scared to speak. "I'm, I'm sorry…" she started.

"Don't be sorry," Issie said. "Be useful." She looked around frantically. "Take off your jacket!' she barked at Kelly-Anne.

"What do you mean?" asked Kelly-Anne.

"Just what I said. Take it off and pass it here."

"What are you going to do with it?" Kelly-Anne asked nervously as she handed the jacket to Issie.

"I'm going to wrap it around Comet's leg like a bandage so he doesn't hurt himself when we pull him out." Issie took off her own jacket too. Then, speaking softly to Comet the whole time, she bent down and wedged her hand through the logs and began to wrap the jackets around his knee and cannon bone. As Issie worked Kelly-Anne watched over her shoulder.

"What now?" Kelly-Anne said. "Do we just make him pull his leg out?"

"No way! We can't move him yet!" Issie said. "The poles are still wedged too close around his leg. We need to open them up a bit so he has enough room to get his hoof out."

Issie looked at the logpile. It had been built solidly like a true cross-country fence. It wasn't going to be easy to pull the logs apart. But the timber logs next to the pony's leg were already broken, so all she really needed was something to push between and lever them apart. Then if she could wedge the logs open another few centimetres, she would be able to get Comet's leg out.

"Give me your riding helmet," ordered Issie. Kelly-Anne didn't hesitate this time. She unbuckled her chin strap and passed Issie the helmet. It was dented in badly on the left side from the fall.

"It probably saved your life," Issie said, showing Kelly-Anne the dent. Then she looked around on the ground. "We need a big stick," she said. "Go and search over there and see if you can find something we can use as a lever to push the logs back while we shove the helmet in the gap. While Issie stood with Comet, reassuring him as she double-checked his bandages, Kelly-Anne searched the ground around the jump.

"How about this?" She lifted up a tree branch. The branch was about two metres long and as thick as her forearm. "Will this do?" Issie took the branch from Kelly-Anne and tried to bend it. The branch didn't yield at all. The wood was green and firm – perfect.

"That should be strong enough," Issie said. "Now," she instructed Kelly-Anne as she shoved the branch at a right angle in between the broken logs, "when I tell you, I want you to lean back on that branch and push down on it as hard as you can. That should prise the logs around Comet's leg apart for a moment. I'm going to shove your riding helmet in between the logs, which will hopefully hold them apart long enough for us to get Comet out."

Issie looked at Kelly-Anne. "Do you understand what you have to do? Are you ready?" The girl nodded.

"OK… now!"

As Kelly-Anne heaved against the branch the logs pulled apart and Issie managed to ram the riding helmet in right next to Comet's trapped leg.

"Keep holding it until I can get the helmet all the way in!" Issie shouted.

"I'm trying!" Kelly-Anne snapped.

As Issie forced the helmet in further, Kelly-Anne's strength faltered and she let go of the stick. There was a horrific cracking noise and Issie was gripped with panic. It sounded like the logs had snapped back and crushed the bones of her horse's leg!

She was relieved to realise it was actually the sound of the hard fibreglass shell of the riding helmet cracking under the pressure. Thankfully the cracked helmet held firm in the gap and the logs remained bowed apart, hopefully just enough for Issie to get Comet's leg out.

The sound of the helmet cracking had startled Comet too and the skewbald pony was now moving about restlessly. "Easy, boy," Issie murmured. "Easy, Comet. I'm going to get you out in just a minute. Steady now…"

There was now room to get both her hands right down into the hole and wrap them tight around Comet's fetlock. Issie lifted the fetlock gently and eased the leg out.

She felt her heart stop when she saw a dark trickle of blood soaking through the jacket that was wrapped around the cannon bone. She told herself to ignore the blood now covering her hands and to focus on getting her horse out. Issie kept lifting the leg, slowly, gently, talking to the quivering skewbald all the time, reassuring him with her voice. It seemed to take forever, but finally she managed to ease Comet's hoof all the way out from between the logs.

"Is he OK?" Kelly-Anne asked.

"I don't know yet," Issie said anxiously as she lowered Comet's hoof back down to the ground. She hastily unwrapped the makeshift bandages to check his leg. There was a lot of blood but the cut on his cannon bone wasn't deep. "I'll have to walk him and see."

As Comet took his first steps forward he seemed reluctant to put any weight at all on the injured leg, holding it up in the air.

"He's lame!" said Kelly-Anne.

"Wait a minute," Issie replied. "He's been stuck in that fence. It's only natural that he's going to favour that leg until he's sure it's OK…"

Sure enough, in a few strides Comet was putting his weight on all four legs again and was walking normally.

When Issie trotted him up to check if he was lame or not, miraculously it looked like the leg was totally sound. The cut on his cannon bone would probably need antibiotic cream, but it seemed to be superficial and other than that the leg was fine. Comet was going to be OK.

"He should be OK to walk home," Issie said with relief.

"Which one of us is going to ride him?" asked Kelly-Anne.

Issie looked at her with astonishment. "The weight of a rider on his back is the last thing Comet needs right now. Neither of us is riding him. You can ride Diablo. I'm going to walk back."

Issie looked up at the sun that was now rising over Lake Deepwater. "It should take us about an hour and a half. We'll take it slow to rest Comet's leg, but we'll still make it home before lunchtime in time for your mum to pick you up."

Kelly-Anne looked even more upset. "Please, Issie." She had tears in her eyes. "I don't want to go home."

"Why not?" said Issie darkly. "You don't seem to like it here much – I would have thought you'd be glad to leave."

Kelly-Anne shook her head. "That's why I ran away on Comet. I thought if Mum came and I wasn't there she'd just give up again and go home. She's going to be so mad at me. Everyone at home is angry all the time. It must be my fault because I know I make people angry. I don't try to, but I do."

Issie looked at Kelly-Anne, who was trying to hide the fact that she was now crying by making a curtain of hair out of her brown bob.

"Kelly-Anne?" Issie said gently. "I think maybe you're the one that's angry. About your parents, I mean. You've been taking it out on the horses since you got here, and on us. But it's not our fault your parents are getting a divorce. And it's not your fault either. These things just happen." Kelly-Anne nodded, but she kept her face hidden under the veil of hair.

"Your mum isn't angry at you. She was really worried about you when Hester said you'd been in trouble," Issie continued. "She told Aunty Hess that things were tough for you at home. And if we'd known what was going on with the divorce and stuff, maybe we wouldn't have been so hard on you."

Kelly-Anne parted her hair away from her face and looked at Issie. "Do I have to go home?"

Issie reached her hand down and helped Kelly-Anne to stand up. "I don't know," she said. "Right now, I think we just need to worry about getting back to the farm before we even think about that."

Kelly-Anne dusted off her jodhpurs and Issie was about to leg her up on to Diablo's back when the girl hesitated. "You got here really quick. How did you do it?"

"What do you mean?"

"I mean, how did you reach us so fast? I was way ahead of you, I must have been. There's no way you could have caught me up."

"I went straight over instead of taking the ridge track," Issie said, pointing back at the steep slope of Blackthorn Hill. Kelly-Anne couldn't believe it.

"But how did you know I was here?" she continued. "How did you know where to come?"

Issie didn't know what to say. She looked over Kelly-Anne's shoulder. There he was, cantering away over the hills in the distance. She smiled as she watched the grey pony, his mane and tail streaming out in the wind. He was almost out of sight now, rounding over the ridge that would take him out of view into the basin of Lake Deepwater. If it hadn't been for Mystic, they would never have made it here in time to save Comet. As for Kelly-Anne, she would never know how Issie had managed to find her that day.

"You were knocked out for a while," Issie told Kelly-Anne. "In fact, I wouldn't be surprised if you didn't have a bit of amnesia!" That seemed to shut Kelly-Anne up. Before the girl could ask any more questions, Issie changed the subject.

"You see that big hill up there to the right? Once we get over that we'll be back on the ridge track. It's all downhill after that. We'll be home in no time."

Issie gave Kelly-Anne a leg-up on to Diablo. Then she picked up Comet's reins and checked the skewbald's leg one more time before they began to head for home.

They had just reached the top of the hill when Issie heard the sound of hoofbeats coming from the other direction and a few moments later Hester and Aidan appeared, cantering around the bend on Stardust and Paris.

"Thank God! Are you both OK?" Hester called out. "Kitty told me everything. Why are you walking? What happened to Comet?" Issie told them the story while Kelly-Anne stood there looking suitably ashamed. The utter stupidity of her actions, taking off with Comet like that, had finally begun to dawn on her.

"Is he lame?" Hester asked.

Issie shook her head. "I don't think so. But I didn't want to ride him back just in case. He took a bad knock when his leg went through the logpile."

Hester looked at Kelly-Anne. "How does your head feel? I'll call ahead now and get the doctor to meet us at the house. He should come and check you for concussion."

"I'm fine, honest," Kelly-Anne said. "I'm really sorry. I know I've caused lots of trouble…"

"Aunty Hess," Issie said, "she really wants to stay. Do you think you could call her mum back and tell her that Kelly-Anne's been given a second chance?"

Kelly-Anne gave Issie a grateful look and then turned to Hester. "Please? I'll make up for everything and I'll do whatever Issie and Stella and Kate tell me to do."

Hester looked doubtful. "We'll talk about this back at the house. Kelly-Anne, are you all right to ride Diablo the whole way?" Kelly-Anne nodded.

"Issie, you can double home with Aidan on Paris and lead Comet," Hester added. "It'll be faster than walking."

Hearing this, Aidan rode forward on Paris. He looked down at Issie but he didn't get off to help her up. Instead, he just took his feet out of his stirrups and lowered a hand for her to grasp. "Slip your foot into my stirrup and I'll swing you up behind me," he said. Issie looked up at Aidan. She didn't return his smile and she didn't take his hand. "Come on, Issie, what are you waiting for?"

Issie wanted to tell him that she was still mad at him over the whole crazy bet he'd made with Dan. She wanted to tell him she knew everything and she thought the boys were both stupid. If Aidan thought that she was going to be his girlfriend because of some silly bet, he was so wrong.

"Issie?" Aidan's smile faltered. "Take my hand."

Issie paused for a moment. Now wasn't the time to talk about it. She had to get Comet home. She put her foot in the stirrup and grasped Aidan's hand tightly. "One-ah-two-ah-three!" Aidan pulled her up, swinging her around so that she was sitting right behind him on Paris's back like a pillion passenger on a motorbike.

Issie kept hold of Comet's reins with her left hand. "Put your arm around me," Aidan instructed her. Issie did as he said, wrapping her arm around Aidan's waist. He was wearing his favourite old tartan shirt. It smelt good, like fresh soap. She let her head rest against his back for a moment and felt the soft flannel of the shirt against her cheek.

"Are you OK back there?" Aidan called over his shoulder.

"Uh-huh."

"Then let's go home."

CHAPTER 14

Issie knew the Horse of the Year was a huge event, but she wasn't prepared for just how huge. There were literally hundreds of horses and riders gathered here at the Gisborne showgrounds. As Avery eased the horse truck across the grass looking for a parking space, the girls gawped out of the windows at the show riders with their glamorous horses tied up to their fabulous, expensive horse trucks.

The horses all had their manes perfectly plaited and their tack polished, and all the riders wore their best sparkling white jods, black or navy hacking jackets and velvet helmets.

"Ohmygod!" Stella squealed. "I just saw Katie McVean! And... I think that blonde girl next to her is Ellen Whitaker! She's from England – I've seen her jumping on TV! Did you see her Issie? Issie?"

Issie didn't say anything. The tingle of excitement that she had felt when they set out from Blackthorn Farm that morning had turned into a tight ball of nerves in her belly. There had been so much drama in the past twenty-four hours, with Comet going missing, that Issie had almost forgotten about entering the pony Grand Prix and the $15,000 first prize.

Yesterday, when they got back to the farm, Issie had wondered if Comet would be sound enough to ride today. Even though the skewbald wasn't favouring his injured leg at all, Issie was still worried. She made a fuss over the pony the moment they got back, cooling his leg using ice packs and dressing the scratch wound to keep any inflammation down. This morning, before they loaded the horses on the truck, Avery had made her trot Comet back and forth down the stable corridor on the hard concrete. Issie was relieved when Avery said he couldn't see any signs of lameness at all and Comet was pronounced fit to compete.

But now that they were actually here at the Horse of the Year, Issie was almost wishing she had an excuse not to ride. She felt totally and utterly sick. What had she been thinking? She was completely out of her league! There was no way she could ride in the Grand Prix.

"Nervous?" Avery looked at her.

"Uh-huh," Issie replied. What she wanted to say was, *Turn the truck around and let's go home – I've changed my mind!*

Avery looked at her as if he understood exactly what she was thinking. "It's pretty daunting, isn't it? When you turn up at a place like this and see the competition."

"Uh-huh."

"Every rider gets nerves, Issie. The great riders are the ones who can put those fears out of their mind and focus on riding and doing their best." Avery smiled. "I wouldn't have brought you here if I didn't think you and Comet were ready for this, would I?"

"No," Issie said uncertainly, "I guess not."

"You may not have a fancy horse truck or a million-dollar horse, Issie, but you've got a pony with talent and the biggest heart I've ever seen," said Avery.

"And besides, you are just as fancy as them. You've got your own groom!" Stella piped up. "That would be me!"

Issie laughed. "Well, in that case," she grinned, "let's do it!"

If Issie's nerves were now gone, well, Comet had

never had any in the first place. The skewbald pony emerged from the truck in the same mood as always – acting as if he owned the place, prancing out of the horse truck with his tail held high and his neck arched like a stallion on parade.

"Comet! Behave!" Issie said as she led him in circles next to the truck trying to calm the little skewbald down.

As Aidan eased Destiny down the ramp of the horse truck and tied him up to the other side he couldn't help laughing at the antics of the skewbald pony. "I don't think Comet has realised that Destiny is actually the stallion here – not him!"

Issie smiled. It was true. Destiny wore a red tag on his bridle today, the mark that a horse was a stallion and that other horses should be wary of getting too close. Stallions were supposed to be watched at all times at horse shows because they might be wild or vicious to other horses. In fact, you couldn't get a more well-mannered horse than Destiny. While Comet skipped and danced about the place, Destiny stood like a perfect gentleman as Aidan unwrapped his floating boots and began to plait up his mane.

Dan, meanwhile, was unloading Madonna from the horse truck and had led her past Issie, tying the chestnut mare up next to Ben's brown gelding Max. He walked around the truck to where Aidan was busy plaiting up the big black horse's forelock.

"Ummm, Aidan?" Aidan looked around and saw who it was.

"Yeah."

Dan put out a hand. "I just want to wish you luck, man." He seemed to mean it as he stuck his hand out.

Aidan too looked like he genuinely wanted to make friends as he grasped Dan's hand and shook it firmly. "Me too. I mean, good luck to you. May the best man win and everything..."

"Do you think they're serious?" Stella said, watching the boys as she stood next to Issie and Comet.

"Uh-huh. Totally," said Issie.

"That is so lame!" Stella giggled. "You have to tell them you know all about their stupid bet. Let them know they can't get away with it!"

"I was going to say something to Aidan yesterday," Issie groaned, "but it was just too embarrassing. It's all so stupid!"

"It's kind of funny though, isn't it?" Stella grinned at Issie. "So, come on. We're best friends, right? And you still haven't even told me – which one do you want to win?"

"That's the whole problem," Issie sighed. "I really don't know."

The Horse of the Year Show had already been underway for two days. Today was considered to be the big day for showjumping, though, with all of the big prize money competitions happening in the main arena.

Dan and Aidan had already reported to the competitors' trailer to get their numbers, which they now wore on their chests. The hacks were jumping first today. Issie would ride in the afternoon in the pony ring.

"They're on in twenty minutes," Stella said, looking at her watch.

"You go ahead to the grandstand and save me a seat," Issie told her. "I'd better go check in at the riders' tent first."

The schedule of the day's events had been posted up on the pinboard outside the competitors' trailer. Issie ran her eyes over the competitor list for the pony Grand Prix to see if she recognised any of the other riders. One of the names on the list leapt out at her. *Ohmygod*, Issie thought. *Just my luck!*

"Well, well, Isadora!" Issie turned around and saw the familiar sour face and stiff blonde plaits of her arch pony-club nemesis – Natasha Tucker!

"Hi, Natasha," Issie said. "I was just checking the competition lists. I see we're both entered in the pony Grand Prix."

Natasha looked at Issie suspiciously. "I didn't even know you were riding at Horse of the Year," she said. "The last time I checked you didn't even have a horse to ride!"

"That's my horse. The skewbald over there," Issie said, pointing to Avery's horse truck where Comet was skipping about and trying to steal hay out of Max's hay net.

"Really?" Natasha tried unsuccessfully to suppress a cruel giggle. "Ewww! A skewbald! They're so ugly! How can you stand to ride him?"

"I think he's beautiful," Issie said, defending Comet. "Anyway, I'm not concerned with how he looks. It's how he jumps that matters."

Natasha sneered. "Well, he doesn't look like Grand Prix material to me!"

"I guess we'll see," said Issie flatly.

"I'm riding the Grand Prix and the Puissance today,"

Natasha continued. "I'm on Fabby, of course. He'll do for this competition, but I'm hoping to pick up a new ride while I'm here as well. You know Ginty McLintoch, don't you? She trains all our horses and Mummy has asked her to keep an eye out for a new pony for me. Mummy says she's willing to spend mega-money on a really special pony that can take me to the Pony-club Champs this year."

"But what will you do with Fabby?" Issie was aghast at the way Natasha chopped and changed ponies as if they were nothing to her.

Natasha ignored this question and looked over Issie's shoulder, her eyes narrowing as she spied Dan mounting up on Madonna next to Avery's horse truck. "Is that Dan?" she asked. Then a slightly bitter tone crept into her voice. "Is he here with you?"

"Uh-huh," Issie said. "He's riding in the next event – novice hack over one metre twenty." Issie paused and then added, "Aidan is riding in it too."

"Ohhh," Natasha said, "I might go and sit in the stands for that. It sounds like it will be worth watching."

"Yes," Issie had to agree, "I guess it will be."

"What is she doing here?" Stella pulled a face as Issie arrived with Natasha in tow and sat down next to Stella and Ben in the grandstand.

"Don't ask!" Issie rolled her eyes.

Kate was in the grandstand too, trying desperately to wrangle the kids. "It's like herding cats!' she grumbled. "They all keep dashing off in different directions!"

"Bottoms on seats now, everyone! You are representing the Blackthorn Farm Riding School – show some manners!" At the sound of Avery's booming voice, Lucy, Sophie, Arthur, George, Tina, Trisha, Kitty and Kelly-Anne all immediately fell silent and sat as still as statues.

"Hi, Issie!' Kelly-Anne beamed up at her, waving furiously. Issie smiled back. She was glad she had managed to convince Aunty Hess to let Kelly-Anne stay on after all.

"I really think she's learnt her lesson this time," Issie had said, standing up for Kelly-Anne. And it seemed that she had. OK, she was still a bit of a know-it-all, but at least she was trying. At their last riding lesson on Saturday, Kelly-Anne hadn't uttered a word and had done everything Kate told her to do. Not only that, she'd helped out with the younger kids too, unsaddling Lucy's horse for her and helping Sophie to mix up Pippen's hard feed after the lesson was over.

"Why isn't Aunty Hess here?" Issie wondered as she looked around. She could have sworn she saw Kate give Stella a strange look at this question.

"Umm, Hess had to go and pick something up. She'll be back soon," Kate said.

There was a crackling noise over the tannoy and then the announcer's voice came through crisp and clear. "The next event in the main arena here today is the novice hack over one metre twenty. This event will be judged on the total points accumulated over two rounds. All riders will complete two rounds."

Issie looked down from the grandstand at the horses warming up below. She could see the boys working in their horses. Dan on Madonna and Aidan on Destiny. She felt a tight knot growing in her tummy.

"I'm going to get an ice cream," Stella said. "Do you want anything?"

"No, thanks," said Issie. "I'm really not hungry."

The knot in Issie's tummy got worse as the competition progressed. Dan and Aidan were the last two riders to go, and so far no one ahead of them had gone clear in the first round.

"It's a difficult course," Avery noted approvingly. "The fences aren't huge, but there are lots of tricky questions for the horses to answer." Avery pointed to the red and white triple that finished the course. "That's the bogey fence," he said. "Hardly anyone has made it clear through that triple."

Issie could barely bring herself to look as Dan rode into the ring on Madonna. The chestnut mare looked stunning, her coat glowing in the sunlight. Dan too looked handsome with his black showjumping jacket and crisp white jodhpurs. As he took the first fence, Madonna tucked her feet up beautifully and cleared it easily, and Issie felt her heart beginning to race. Would Dan go clear? It certainly looked like he might as he took the second, third and fourth fences with ease. As Madonna approached the double she did a funny stride and then had to pop in an extra stride at the middle of the fence, which meant that she bashed her hind legs on the rails.

The crowd held their breath, but the rail didn't fall. Dan was still clear. Over the next three fences too his luck held. Now all that was left was the triple. Madonna approached the triple with a perfect stride, ah-one she was over the first fence, ah-two and the second, ah… no! There was a collective sigh of disappointment from the crowd, who were hoping that this would be the first clear round of the day. Instead, Madonna managed to knock the very last rail with her front legs and down it came. Four faults!

"That still keeps him in the front running," Ben said, watching intently. "And there's only Aidan to come."

Aidan looked tense as he brought Destiny into the ring. Issie could see that Destiny was straining against the reins, making it hard for Aidan to hold him and get his striding right between fences.

As they came through the start flags Issie saw Aidan check the black horse firmly to let him know he meant business. Destiny arched his neck and his canter became bouncy and forward as he popped neatly over the first fence. The crowd clapped as Destiny took the second, third and fourth fences with ease and then romped over the double as if it wasn't even there. By the time Aidan came down the final line to face the triple, he hadn't knocked down a single rail. If he went clear through the triple then he would be the only rider to make it through the first round with no faults.

Issie held her breath as Aidan took the last turn into the triple a little too tightly, not leaving himself much time at all to settle Destiny into a steady stride before the first fence. Destiny seemed to manage it though. The black horse took the first fence... one, then two... he was clear so far. You could hear the silence as the crowd waited to see whether he would make it over the last fence – and then came the thunderous applause as the black horse cleared the final fence and raced through the finish flags. Destiny had gone clear! Aidan had done it.

The man on the tannoy crackled back into life again. "Aidan MacGuire on Blackthorn Destiny goes clear, putting him out in the lead as we enter the second round." He explained, "So with four riders sitting just behind Aidan MacGuire on four faults each, we still have a real battle on our hands!"

"Can Dan still win?" Stella whispered to Issie.

"Uh-huh," Issie said. "He's only got four faults. It's accumulated points and there's still one more round to come."

The jump-off course had been tightened down to eight fences and, as was the tradition in these events, the rider with the worst score from the last round rode first. That meant the leader from the last round, Aidan, would be riding last.

As the riders took their second round it became clear that, once again, the triple fence was the bogey. None of the riders seemed to manage a clear round. Then it was Dan's turn. Issie watched as he circled Madonna around in a warm-up lap.

"Go, Dan!" Ben shouted from the stands as Madonna came through the start flags and positively flew over the first fence. The kids were shouting out too, cheering every time Dan went clear over a fence. Issie, meanwhile, sat quietly watching. She wanted Dan to do well – of course she did. But did she want him to beat Aidan and win the bet?

As Dan lined up for the final triple she felt her heart catch in her throat. Madonna took the first fence beautifully, and the second and… as Dan cleared the third fence for a clear round Issie heard the crowd go crazy. Dan had done it! He had gone clear!

"Now this makes the competition interesting!" boomed the tannoy man. "Dan Halliday has gone clear in the second round. That means our last rider, Aidan MacGuire, has to go clear also with no time faults. If he collects a single rail, he will slip back in the rankings to equal Dan Halliday. If he takes two rails, he'll fall behind Dan to second place!"

The tension showed on Aidan's face as he brought Destiny back into the ring. Aidan nodded to the judges and heard the bell that signalled that he could start. He pushed Destiny into a canter and the black horse took the first fence with a clean take-off, clearing it neatly.

"Go, Aidan!" Kate, Stella and the kids were shouting their heads off now as Aidan took Destiny over fence after fence without a fault.

As Aidan turned to face the triple Issie felt her heart pounding. She had been so confused for so long about Dan and Aidan that she didn't know what to think. Now, as Aidan lined up to take the final jump, suddenly her heart made up her mind for her. She realised she had been jumping with Aidan over every single fence. Wishing him over the jumps. At that moment, she knew at last how she really felt.

"Go, Aidan!" she yelled so loudly that Stella and Natasha, who were sitting next to her, nearly jumped out of their skins.

Aidan looked at the triple ahead of him and managed to judge his stride perfectly at the first fence. Then trouble struck. Destiny miscued his take-off for the second fence and took down a rail. The error left him disunited as he approached the third fence and the top rail fell from that one too. There was a collective sigh from the crowd as the man on the tannoy crackled back to life.

"A very unlucky eight faults there for Aidan MacGuire, putting him back to second place. That makes our winner of the one metre twenty novice hack event… Mr Dan Halliday on Madonna! Second place is Aidan MacGuire on Blackthorn Destiny and third goes to Justin Jones on Tribesman. Would all the riders come into the arena for prize-giving please?"

"Issie?" Stella looked at her friend. "Are you OK?"

Issie shook her head. She wasn't OK at all. Dan had won. Aidan had lost. Issie had finally made up her mind and she knew what she wanted… she knew who she wanted. And now it was too late.

CHAPTER 15

Issie wasn't even looking at Dan and Madonna as they took their victory lap around the arena. Her eyes never left Aidan. From the grandstand she watched as he slid down off his horse. She saw him quietly whisper something to the black stallion as he stroked his muzzle, as if horse and rider were consoling each other over their loss.

Then she saw Aidan look away from Destiny and up at the grandstand, his eyes searching for Issie. At that moment he looked so heartbroken, so miserable, that Issie realised she couldn't stand it any longer. She had to talk to him! She stood up and began to move towards the exit.

"Hey! What's going on? Where are you going?" Stella said as Issie pushed past her. "Issie? What's happening?"

Issie stopped and turned to Stella. "It's all wrong. I wanted Aidan to win."

Stella looked confused. "But, Issie, if you wanted Aidan to win then why didn't you just choose him in the first place?"

"Because I didn't know I wanted him to win until just now!" Issie replied.

"What's going on?" Arthur piped up.

"Issie wanted Aidan to win!" said Kitty.

"But why?" Lucy asked.

"Issie, is Aidan your boyfriend?" asked Sophie.

"Yes. I mean no... I mean, he should be. Ummm... Stella, can you get them some more ice creams? I gotta go!" Issie hurdled the back of the bench seats and began to run along a vacant row of seating towards the grandstand door. The only person she wanted to talk to right now was Aidan. She had to tell him how she really felt about him.

She was almost back to Avery's horse truck, making her way there as fast as she could by darting in and out between the other trucks and floats, when she heard a voice beside her. "Hey, Issie!"

It was Dan. He was on Madonna and he had a huge smile on his face. Madonna looked pleased with herself too. She was dancing about, the gold tassels of her red winner's sash flapping against her chest as she moved.

"Did you see the jump-off?" Dan asked as he slid down off Madonna's back and landed on the ground next to her.

"Yeah, I did," Issie said. "Ummm… you jumped brilliantly. It was a really good round and you deserved to win."

Dan looked at her face and suddenly his smile disappeared. "So why do I get the feeling that you're not happy that I won then?" he said.

Issie looked at Dan. She couldn't speak – she was finding it hard enough just to breathe! *You have to do this*, she told herself. Dan didn't deserve to be messed around. Now that she knew how she felt about him and Aidan, she had to say something…

"I know about the bet."

"What?" Dan looked nervous.

"You and Aidan. I heard you. I was in the horse truck when you were talking and I heard you…"

Dan froze like a rabbit in the headlights. Issie knew about the bet! "I never really meant it!" he babbled. "It was just a silly thing to say. You didn't think I really expected you to be my girlfriend, did you?" Then he looked at her. "That is, unless you want to. Be my girlfriend, I mean."

Issie looked at Dan. "Dan, I... can't."

It felt awful that moment. The crushed look on Dan's face, the desperate hot flush of embarrassment as he tried to act cool, as if he didn't care that she had turned him down.

"I was just being silly. I didn't mean it..." he said again. He avoided meeting her eyes by busying himself with adjusting Madonna's martingale.

"I'm sorry," Issie said softly.

"Hey, I said I never meant it, all right?" Dan said, still refusing to look at her. "Don't worry about it, OK?" He put his foot back in the stirrup and sprang up on to Madonna's back. "I gotta go. I need to get to the judges' tent and collect my prize money: $10,000! Can you believe it?"

Issie shook her head. She wanted to say something, anything that would make things the way that they used to be between them, but she didn't know what to say. "Dan, I..."

"Anyway," Dan said coolly, turning Madonna so that he had his back to Issie, "I'll see you later."

Issie watched helplessly as he rode away. Dan trotted

off for a few strides and then something made him stop and pull Madonna up to a halt. He turned back to her. "Issie?"

"Uh-huh?"

"Good luck, OK? For the pony Grand Prix." He smiled at her. "I really hope you win."

Issie smiled back. "Thanks, Dan."

"Do it for the Chevalier Point Pony Club!" He gave her a wave, then he turned Madonna again and trotted away.

Issie stood there for a moment watching him ride off. It might take a while to get totally back to normal, but she knew now that things were going to be OK between her and Dan. It had been good to talk to him. But now all she really wanted was to find Aidan and…

"Isadora! There you are! I've been looking all over for you!" Aunt Hester was striding over the showgrounds towards her. She was wearing her best black jodhpurs and a pink shirt and carrying a large picnic basket.

"I've brought a surprise with me," Hester said. At first Issie thought her aunt was referring to the picnic basket, and she was so busy staring at it that she didn't notice the woman with long dark hair and a broad smile on her face who was walking just behind Hester.

"Hello, sweetie!"

"Mum?" Issie couldn't believe it!

"Mum! Ohmygod! What are you doing here?" she squealed as she ran to Mrs Brown and gave her the most enormous hug.

"What? Do you think I'd miss the chance to see my daughter ride in the pony Grand Prix?" Mrs Brown laughed.

"I just picked your mum up from the airport this morning," Hester explained.

Issie still didn't believe it. Her mum was here!

"I fed your horses their breakfast and then I got on the plane," Mrs Brown said breezily.

"Are they OK?" asked Issie.

"Blaze and Storm are fine," Mrs Brown said. "I asked Pip at the pony club to keep an eye on them until I get back."

"I'm so glad you came!" Issie grinned.

"Hess says you're riding just before lunch?"

"Uh-huh. I was just on my way back to the horse truck now. I suppose I should start getting him ready."

"Well, come on then!" said Mrs Brown. "I've heard so much about Comet. I think it's time I met this superstar pony of yours."

Issie was still desperate to talk to Aidan. She had been hoping that he would be back at the horse truck with Destiny when she got there, but they were nowhere in sight.

"I think he had another class to ride in," Stella said as she reached the truck to join them.

Issie wanted to go and find him, but with her mother here and the time ticking by until her competition started, she figured that her conversation with Aidan would have to wait. It was time to get ready to ride.

"All you have to worry about is getting yourself dressed," Stella told her. "I'm your groom, remember."

"Yeah, but…"

"Hey!" Stella said. "I've got it covered, OK? I can look after Comet. I've even got myself an assistant."

"An assistant?"

"Hi, Isadora!" Issie looked over Stella's shoulder and saw Kelly-Anne standing nervously to the side of the horse truck. "Stella said I could help her get Comet ready… if it's OK with you?"

Issie looked at her. "Do you know how to do gamgee bandages?"

Kelly-Anne shook her head. "No, I don't."

Issie smiled. "That's OK. This is a good chance for you to learn how to do them properly. Stella will teach you how to put them on."

"Here," Stella said, passing Kelly-Anne a roll of bandages and a wadge of stuff that looked a bit like cotton wool. "I'll do the first one and then you can copy me and do the next one, OK?"

Issie left them to it and went inside the horse truck to get changed. She pulled on her white jodhpurs and long black boots. She opened the closet and stared at her riding jacket. It wasn't actually hers – it was an old one of Hester's. It was a little bit big for her and a tad moth-eaten, but it didn't really matter. It would have to do.

Issie was just slipping off her T-shirt and putting on her shirt when there was a knock at the door of the horse truck and her mum stepped inside. She was holding a black box tied with a black and white grosgrain ribbon.

"Before you put that old jacket on, you might want to open this." Mrs Brown smiled as she passed the box to Issie. It was filled with lilac tissue paper, and beneath the tissue there was a brand-new navy blue riding jacket.

"Oh, Mum! It's gorgeous!" Issie couldn't believe it.

"When you phoned me the other night for the entry money, I realised that you didn't have a showing jacket to wear," Mrs Brown said. "So I called Hester and asked her what I should get you."

"Thank you!" beamed Issie.

"There's a tie in there with it," Mrs Brown pointed out. "A navy jacket and a red tie. The Chevalier Point colours. I thought they'd bring you luck."

Issie pulled the jacket out of its tissue paper. The navy fabric was so dark it almost looked black. The jacket had a velvet collar, also in navy blue, and a single vent up the back. It was a classic showjumper's jacket.

"I hope it fits," Mrs Brown said. "You're growing so fast these days I find it hard to tell what size you are!" Issie slipped on the navy jacket and did up the buttons. It was a perfect fit.

"Thanks, Mum!" she grinned. Then her face fell. "But I already owe you $500! And now this jacket…"

Mrs Brown smiled. "The jacket is a gift. And don't worry about the $500."

"But if I don't win this event then I won't be able to pay you back or help Aunty Hess with the farm…"

"Issie, you're only fourteen. That's far too young

to take the weight of the world on your shoulders," Mrs Brown said firmly. "You need to put all of that out of your mind. All I want is for you to go out there and do your best and have fun, OK? That's all anyone is asking of you."

"OK, Mum." Despite what her mother said, Issie was still feeling the butterflies beginning to churn in her tummy. There was $15,000 in prize money up for grabs in this event. If she won then she could give the money to Hester and maybe she wouldn't have to sell the farm and… Issie tried to put those thoughts out of her mind. Her mum was right. She had to focus on riding, not winning.

Mrs Brown looked at her watch. "It's nearly eleven," she said. "I'm going to go with Hester now and get a good seat in the stands. I'll see you afterwards."

As her mother opened the door of the truck Issie called after her. "Mum?"

"Yes?"

"I'll try to make you proud of me."

There were tears in Mrs Brown's eyes as she looked at Issie. "Oh, honey, I'm already proud of you. I always have been." She gave Issie one last hug. "Here, let me straighten your tie… perfect!"

She looked at Issie and smiled. "Now get out there and good luck!"

The grandstand was already crowded as Mrs Brown, Hester, Stella, Kate and the kids hurried to their seats.

"With $15,000 at stake this is one of the premier pony events in the Southern hemisphere," the announcer's voice crackled over the loudspeaker.

"$15,000? That's big money!" Stella gave a low whistle.

"Yeah, big jumps too! Look!" Kate pointed down at the arena. "They're huge."

In the warm-up arena down below, Issie was looking at the ring and thinking exactly the same thing. "Tom?" She looked nervously at Avery, who was holding on to Comet's reins as he gave her some last-minute advice.

"Take a deep breath and take your time," her instructor said. "Remember, the main thing is a clear round; speed doesn't matter in this event." Issie nodded.

"And watch the turn into that last double," Avery added. "Don't take it too tight on the corner! Remember what happened to that last rider – it's a big fence: you need three decent strides to take it."

Issie nodded and turned Comet towards the arena. She was the last rider to go, which put her in a lucky position. Earlier, she had watched Natasha come in and put in a nice round on Fabergé, with just one rail down for four faults. The fences were challenging, and there had been only one other rider who had done better than Natasha and gone clear. If Issie got a rail down, she'd have four faults too, just like Natasha. But if she went clear, she'd be ahead of Natasha and in the jump-off for first place.

The grandstands were packed and there was a round of applause from the crowd as Issie cantered into the ring. Issie nearly lost control as Comet bolted forward at the sound of their clapping, yanking the reins clean out of her hands. She managed to grab at the reins and had to pull hard to get Comet to a halt. As they stood in the arena she realised that the pony was actually trembling beneath her. "Easy, Comet," she soothed him. "What's wrong?"

She didn't have a chance to find out. There was a loud clang as the bell rang, signalling the start of the round. According to the rules, that meant Issie now had only one minute to get her horse through the flags and start her round or she would be disqualified. The clock was ticking. She had to ride now.

"Come on, Comet." Issie worked the skewbald in a canter circle to try to settle him then took a perfect line over the first fence. Comet seemed to relax again and took the fence nicely, tucking his feet up and clearing the rails, but as he landed on the other side the crowd let out a cheer and their cries made Comet surge forward again in a panic.

"Comet!" Issie tried to hold him, but the skewbald was too strong for her. He was rushing his fences and refusing to settle into a steady stride. Every time Issie lined him up for a jump Comet would hear the crowd cheering him on and lose his cool and charge the fence. She was lucky to make it over the first half of the course, but by the time they hit the big oxer in the middle of the course Issie knew they were in trouble. Comet rushed it so fast that his striding was all wrong, and he took off in a flying leap way, way earlier than he should have done. Issie squealed in shock as the pony jumped too soon. Instead of coming down on the other side of the fence, Comet brought his hind legs down on the back half of the jump, scattering poles everywhere.

The skewbald kept cantering on, but Issie was now

terrified. He was totally out of control. Issie's fears were instinctively picked up on by Comet. As he reached the next jump he panicked and screeched to a halt in front of the fence at the last minute, baulking to one side. Issie hadn't been expecting this. Comet had never refused a jump before! She was thrown forward on to the skewbald's neck and nearly fell off. She had to grapple her way back along his neck and into the saddle like a gymnast to avoid the twenty faults she would have got for a fall. But once she was back in the saddle she realised it didn't matter anyway. She already had four faults for a rail down and four for a refusal – plus her horse was shaking so much there was no way she was going to make it around the rest of the course.

Issie looked up at the judges' tent and slowly raised her riding crop up to her helmet in a salute.

"What's she doing?" Mrs Brown asked Kate. "Why is she saluting in the middle of the course like that?"

Kate looked down at Issie from the grandstand. She couldn't believe it. "She's retiring. That salute means that she's just quit. She's out!"

"That was an unfortunate round for pony Grand Prix newcomer Isadora Brown and Blackthorn Comet," the announcer said. "She has retired from the competition and is out of the running for the $15,000."

Issie was devastated as she left the arena. All that training, all those hopes of saving the farm – and now here they were, eliminated in the first round!

Comet had calmed down as soon as they left the arena and the noise of the crowd had died down, but Issie was still shaking from the experience. This had been it. Their big event. How could it have all gone so wrong?

As she walked Comet around to cool the pony down Avery rushed over towards her. Issie shook her head miserably as she saw her instructor approaching as if to say, *I know, it's my fault, I messed up*.

"Having a few problems in there?" asked Avery.

"I guess I panicked, Tom," Issie said. "Comet got spooked by the crowds and then I couldn't concentrate and it all kind of fell apart and…"

"It's not your fault, Issie," Avery said. "I'm kicking myself. I should have thought about it earlier. It's the noise of the crowd. Comet's not used to it. I should have thought of this before you went in there. But at least it's not too late to fix it."

He put his hand into his pocket and pulled out what looked like a crocheted doily, the sort that sits on your nan's bedside table. Issie noticed that there was something unusual about the doily – it appeared to have two pointy bits in the middle of it.

"It's an ear net," Avery explained as he began to fit the doily over Comet's ears. "It will muffle the sound and cut out the crowd noise."

"Will it really work?"

"It should do," Avery said. "Lots of professional riders use them to block out the crowd noise and help their horses to focus. I'm betting that Comet's problems in the ring just now were purely because he's not used to all that racket." Avery patted the skewbald on his white striped face." Anyway, there's only one way to find out."

Issie was confused. "But, Tom, it's too late. The pony Grand Prix is over. I've withdrawn."

Avery looked at her, "Well, yes and no."

"What do you mean?"

"I've entered you in another event." Issie couldn't believe it.

"What?"

"The pony Puissance," Avery said.

"But, Tom. Why? It must have cost you $500! You're

going to lose your money! You saw him in the ring just now! It was a disaster!"

Avery put his hand on Comet's neck and looked up at her. "Issie, the Puissance is a completely different event. It requires a pony with exceptional bravery, and a rider who can put all their trust in their horse." He looked at her. "Comet can do this. I know he can – that's why I paid your entry."

Comet lifted his head up as Avery said this, as if he knew that they were talking about him. Issie looked at his bold chestnut and white face. Avery was right – Comet had more courage than any pony she had ever met. If they quit now, she would never know what he was really capable of.

"OK, Tom," she nodded. "We'll do it."

Avery smiled at her. "Excellent. The competition begins in an hour. That gives us enough time for a quick lesson in showjumping Puissance-style."

Comet, who seemed to realise that something was going on, began to dance beneath her. "Steady, Comet," Issie soothed him. "You're getting a second chance in that ring, boy," she whispered. "We both are."

A sense of determination gripped Issie now as she turned to her instructor. "We're ready," she said. "Let's go."

CHAPTER 16

Issie felt her tummy tighten with nerves. The Puissance had begun, but there were several other riders to go before it was her turn in the ring. Issie kind of wished she was going first. It would have been easier in a way to get it over and done with. That way you didn't have a chance to get nervous. As Avery gave her some last-minute advice on jumping technique she tried to listen, but it was hard to concentrate. As she looked at the jumps in the arena her mind kept going back to her round in the Grand Prix. It had been a total disaster! And now she was going back into the ring to face the biggest jumps of her life? This was crazy!

"The key," Avery was telling her, "is to get your horse in quite deep to the fence to get a good bascule over the jump." He put down his riding crop about two metres out from the practice jump. "Imagine that this crop marks your take-off point," he said.

Issie looked at the practice jump which Avery had fixed at a metre forty. To Issie, even the practice jump looked utterly huge.

"I've never jumped that high before," she said.

"Yes, you have!" Avery said. "Remember the Puissance training that we did at home? Comet took one metre forty easily. We never got the chance to see how much higher he could go, but I think he can do even better than that. I think he can win this event."

"Uh-huh," Issie said, sounding unconvinced.

Avery looked her in the eyes. He could see now that something was wrong. "Are you nervous?"

"A little," Issie admitted.

Avery nodded. "It's perfectly normal to be nervous. But somehow you need to lose your fears before you enter that arena. Showjumping is all about keeping your cool."

"I know, Tom," said Issie. "It's just that when Comet got spooked in the arena in the Grand Prix and I nearly fell off, I guess I kind of lost my nerve a bit…"

"He was only panicking because of the noise, Issie," Avery said.

"I know, I know, and he has the ear net now and everything... but, Tom, those are big jumps in there!"

Avery looked at her. "Comet is a very smart horse. He knows exactly what you're feeling. If you panic then he'll panic too. If you relax then he'll relax. Do you understand?"

Relax! Issie looked across the arena at the crowded grandstand. "Yeah, right! How can I? This is the Horse of the Year pony Puissance!"

Avery looked at her intently. "Take a deep breath and listen to me," he said. "You had a rough ride in the Grand Prix, but you and I both know that Comet can do this. He's a superstar, Issie. You have to give him the chance to prove it."

Issie took a deep breath and slowly let it out again. In her heart, she knew Avery was right. Comet was a star. Hadn't Issie known that from the very first day they met? Avery saw it straightaway too. Even Mystic knew it. Wasn't that why Mystic had been watching over Comet ever since Issie arrived at Blackthorn Farm? Mystic had helped her to find the skewbald pony that day when Kelly-Anne had taken him. Mystic believed in Comet. Now, after all they had been through, maybe it was time for Issie to make a final leap of faith and truly believe in this horse too.

Issie took another deep breath and this time, as she exhaled, she willed herself to be brave, to trust absolutely in her horse. She felt the butterflies in her belly dissolve as she breathed all the nervous energy out and took another new breath in again.

"Are you ready?" Avery said.

"Yes, Tom," she smiled. "I'm ready – and so is Comet."

"We're up to competitor number twenty in the pony Puissance," the announcer called. "Isadora Brown on Blackthorn Comet."

As she rode through into the arena and looked at the first fence Issie felt a tingle up her spine. Not from nerves this time, but from excitement. She wanted to do this.

"Come on, Comet," she whispered to her pony. "You and I know you're the best jumper here – and now we're gonna prove it to them."

With his smart new ear net on, Comet was no longer bothered by the crowd noise. The pony was totally unfazed and every inch the showjumper as Issie worked him around in a bouncy canter and headed towards the first fence. Comet took the painted rails with ease, flicking up his heels as he went over and giving a grunt of satisfaction as he landed on the other side as if to say, *Piece of cake!*

"Steady, boy." Issie turned him and gathered him up again for the brick wall. Even though she knew it was just made of wooden blocks, it looked really solid and scary. She swallowed her nerves and felt a surge of power from beneath her as Comet pricked his ears forward at the fence and approached it in a rounded canter, with one stride... two... three strides and over! They had gone clear! The crowd clapped politely. It was only the first round. Most of the thirty young riders competing in this event would go clear in this round. But there were still four rounds to go after this – and with each round, the brick wall would grow.

"The field stewards are now raising the wall to one metre forty," the announcer told the crowd in the grandstand.

The second round was far more dramatic than the first. One metre forty was enough to knock out quite a few competitors. By the time the wall was raised again for round three, there were only eight riders left.

The loudspeaker crackled back to life. "The wall is

now being set at one metre fifty," the announcer called.

"One metre fifty? You might as well give up now! You'll never make it over that on your ugly skewbald!" Issie turned around to see Natasha Tucker pouting at her from the back of her grey pony Fabergé.

"Did you see me and Fabby in that last round?" Natasha said. "Fabby just flew over the fence. Puissance is his speciality." She looked darkly at Issie. "I really do expect to win this."

Issie couldn't believe it. Of all the people to be in a jump-off with, did she have to be riding against Stuck-up Tucker?

Natasha's smugness got even worse a few moments later when she rode the next round and Fabergé went clear over the one metre fifty wall. Issie watched Natasha ride out of the ring with an unbearably pleased-with-herself look. She wasn't the only one to go clear. Three other riders had already made it round and the pressure was really on.

Avery's last-minute advice for getting over the wall this time was short and to the point. "Don't think about it too hard," he said to Issie as she entered the ring. "Just jump it!"

Comet did exactly that. Issie came into the ring, popped neatly over the painted rails and then turned

Comet to face the wall. She counted his strides out loud under her breath to keep herself focused. "One, two, three!" As the skewbald took off this time Issie realised just how big the fence was. One metre fifty! That was as tall as she was! She had just jumped herself!

For the fourth round the fence went up to one metre sixty. Issie looked at the brick wall and tried not to get freaked out. She was pretty sure now that the wall was so tall Comet wouldn't even be able to see over it.

"We're down to the final two rounds," the announcer said. "With only five riders left, it remains to be seen who will make it over this wall and into the jump-off for the final round."

Issie looked at the four other riders. She couldn't believe she had made it so far. She was in the fourth round. If she could get over the fence this time then she would make the final jump-off.

She looked over at Natasha Tucker. Natasha was circling Fabergé outside the arena now under the watchful eye of a horse-faced woman with long flame-red hair and tan jodhpurs.

"Who's she?" Issie asked.

"You really don't know?" Avery was surprised. "Issie, that's Ginty McLintoch. She's trained some of the best showjumping riders. She has some of the best horses in her stable too." Avery pointed at Natasha's grey pony Fabergé. "The word is that Ginty charged the Tuckers top dollar for Fabergé. She's renowned for having a real eye for horse flesh. Ginty has customers who are willing to pay big bling for a talented pony…"

The loudspeaker crackled back into life. "We're in the fourth round of the pony Puissance here at the Horse of the Year with Natasha Tucker on Fabergé next into the arena."

Issie watched as Natasha rode into the ring. Natasha's eyes were set at the jumps with steely determination. Issie had noticed that she brandished a hot pink riding crop in the previous rounds. This time when Natasha was a couple of strides out from the wall she used the crop, bringing it down hard against Fabergé's flank and screaming, "Get up!"

Poor Fabergé looked thoroughly shocked at being hit for no reason and his canter became disunited, but he managed to take off cleanly somehow and still cleared the wall.

Avery shook his head. "That's a classic Ginty McLintoch rider for you," he sighed. "Ginty trains all her students to use their whips as soon as the fences get big."

"Actually, I don't think Natasha needs any encouragement when it comes to using her whip," said Issie. She watched Natasha ride back out of the arena with a huge grin on her face. And Natasha's grin got even wider a few minutes later when the next three riders all failed to make it over the wall.

"Only one rider has made it over the wall so far. Now it's time for our last competitor, Isadora Brown on Blackthorn Comet," the announcer said.

As Issie took Comet into the ring this time she tried to remember everything Avery had told her about bringing the pony in deep to the fence and not holding him back. As she popped Comet over the painted rails she felt the pony arc up beneath her and she knew for certain as she turned to face the wall that Comet was ready to do this.

Up in the grandstand above her, though, the others weren't so sure.

"Ohmygod!" Stella squealed. "That wall is totally huge!"

"I can't look!" Kate had her hands over her face and was peering through her fingers.

"Is it safe for her to jump a wall that size?" Mrs Brown asked Hester.

"You must be joking!" Hester said without thinking. Then she saw Mrs Brown's distraught face and added, "She'll be fine, Amanda. She'll get over it no trouble – you watch!"

"Come on, Issie!" Tina, Trisha, Lucy, Sophie, Kitty, Kelly-Anne, George and Arthur were screaming at the top of their lungs.

Down in the arena, Comet's ears swivelled as he heard the shouts of the crowd. But the ear net had muffled the noise and he didn't lose his cool. Neither did Issie as she lined the skewbald pony up to the wall, took a deep breath and rode him forward at a fast canter. Comet took four big strides and then leapt straight up in the air. It almost looked like the pony was climbing the wall rather than jumping it as he rose up and over. Then he did a neat flip with his hindquarters, flicking his fetlocks up in the air so that they too flew above the bricks.

"Is she over?" Kate asked, peeking through her fingers. "Did she do it?" Her question was answered by the roar of the crowd going wild. Issie was clear!

"We are down to just two competitors in the final round. Natasha Tucker on Fabergé and Isadora Brown on Blackthorn Comet," the announcer said. "The course stewards are now raising the wall. They've taken it up another ten centimetres this time. That means final height for our pony Puissance today will be one metre seventy!"

As the stewards added another row of bricks to raise the height of the wall, Issie tried to stay calm and keep Comet working at a trot around the warm-up area. A metre seventy! *It's OK*, she told herself, *that's just ten more centimetres, hardly anything at all. Comet can do it.*

"Issie!" A voice called out to her. She looked up and saw Natasha Tucker riding towards her on Fabby. There was something wrong though. Issie couldn't place it at first and then she realised what it was. Natasha was smiling at her.

"Issie!" Natasha said. "I just wanted to ask you something. It's just that, well, the ground is quite hard and I don't want to hurt Fabby's legs more than I have to and I was just wondering… well…"

"What?" said Issie.

"I was just wondering if you want to call it quits at round four," Natasha said. "We could tell the judges that we're both stopping now and then they'd call a draw and we'd both share the first and second prize money." Natasha gave Issie a smile. "What do you think? Do we have a deal?"

Issie looked at the wall. Maybe Natasha was right. An extra ten centimetres meant that the wall was totally huge now. Way bigger than anything she had ever jumped in her life. She looked back at Natasha, and then she remembered what Avery had said about horses being able to sense fear. At that moment, Issie could sense it too. She realised that Natasha was afraid. Afraid of the wall and afraid of losing to Issie. That was the difference between these two riders now. Sure, the wall was huge, but Issie still believed she could do it. She believed that Comet could jump it. And she wasn't afraid. She was ready.

"Thanks, Natasha, but I want to ride," she said. "I want to see how this one turns out."

Natasha's smile instantly transformed into a scowl. "Your loss," she said. "Just remember I gave you your chance to be a winner, OK?"

"Natasha Tucker on Fabergé into the ring please!" the announcer called.

"Good luck, Natasha," Issie said.

"What-ever!" Natasha snapped back as she turned Fabergé and rode into the arena. The steely determination was still there on Natasha's face, but this time as she took the first fence and turned to face the wall, Issie saw something else in there as well.

Fabergé sensed the change in his rider too. As they came in to take the wall this time, Issie could only just see the very tips of the grey pony's ears above the wall. She saw Fabergé approach and then get ready to take off and then, at the very last moment, Natasha lashed out with her whip. At the same time, though, she stiffened and hesitated and Fabergé felt the conflict of being struck by this girl who was afraid to go over the wall. Instinctively, the horse became afraid too. Instead of leaping, at the very last moment he planted his feet and slid to a stop. Natasha, who hadn't been expecting this, flew clean over his head and straight into the wall. There was a loud gasp from the crowd as the bricks and rider all tumbled down in a great heap, and then a sigh of relief when Natasha stood up and dusted herself off.

"And unfortunately for Natasha Tucker and Fabergé that fall means disqualification in the final round," the announcer said. "Our stewards are just taking a few moments to rebuild the wall and then we'll have our last competitor, Isadora Brown on Blackthorn Comet."

In the grandstand the crowd went completely silent as Issie entered the ring.

Comet seemed to know that every eye in the place was on him. The little skewbald had always known he was a star, and now that he had his moment to show them, he was loving it! Issie could feel the fizzing tension in his chestnut and white body. The little horse was almost trembling with excitement and eagerness as he took the painted rails with ease and came around the corner for the last time to confront the wall.

As Issie approached the wall this time she tried to clear her mind. *Don't think about how big it is,* she told herself, *and don't think about the danger. Just think about being on the other side.*

Professional showjumpers will tell you that once the fences start getting really big, jumping feels totally different. There is a moment when it doesn't feel like you are jumping at all; it feels like you are flying. It felt like that now as Comet took the wall. As the pony leapt up and up, Issie felt the world fall away behind her, and then she was in midair. As they crested the top of the wall it felt like they were in slow motion, floating there for a moment, before they came down the other side.

This time, all the ear nets in the world couldn't have muffled the noise of the crowd. The grandstand went wild with applause as the little skewbald landed on the other side. They were clear. They had won!

"Isadora Brown and Blackthorn Comet are the winners of the pony Puissance!" the announcer called. "A fantastic jump at one metre seventy and a well-deserved win for the prize of the Puissance Cup!"

"I get a cup?" Issie couldn't believe it. "Tom, did you hear that? I get a cup!"

"You get more than that," Avery beamed at her.

"What do you mean?"

"Issie, you just won $15,000!"

"What?" Issie couldn't believe it. She had assumed there would be some prize money for the Puissance, but she had never dreamt it would be that much! "Why didn't you tell me I was jumping for that much money?"

"Because it would have made you nervous," Avery said. "I figured you were coping with your nerves quite well. I didn't want to say anything that might throw you."

"Ohmygod!" Issie still couldn't believe it.

"Go on!" Avery grinned at her. "Get into the ring for prize-giving!"

Issie had to laugh as they took their victory lap of the arena with their trophy and the red sash tied around Comet's neck. This was Comet's moment and boy did the skewbald know it. He pranced about the ring with his neck arched and his head high as if to say, *I told you all that I could do it, didn't I?*

As they cantered out of the arena, the whole gang from Blackthorn Farm was on the sidelines to meet them.

"Mum!" Issie jumped down off her horse and gave her mother a huge hug. "We did it!"

"Wasn't he a superstar out there?" Mrs Brown said.

Issie hugged Comet tight around his neck. The pony wouldn't stay still though; he was still prancing about, making the most of all the attention.

"Comet, I can see you are going to be completely unbearable to live with from now on!" Issie giggled.

Hester sighed. "Isadora, he was already unbearable before. I can see that I'm going to have to build some paddocks with bigger fences when we get him home."

"That might not be necessary," said the woman striding towards her. Issie recognised the red hair and tan jodhpurs immediately. It was the same woman she had seen training Natasha Tucker. It was Ginty McLintoch.

"Hello, Hester," the red-headed woman said briskly.

"Hello, Ginty," Hester said. "I suppose you've come over to see our Puissance champion?"

"I've come to do more than that," Ginty said. "I've come to buy him."

"What makes you think he's for sale?"

Ginty looked Hester in the eye. "Don't play games, Hester. Everyone knows your farm is in trouble. I imagine that a cash injection from a horse sale is just what you need right now, and I'm here to offer it to you."

"He's not for sale, Ginty," Hester replied coolly.

"Oh, really?" Ginty raised an eyebrow and took out her chequebook. She smiled at Hester. "I've got a cheque here for $25,000 that says that he is."

Issie looked at her aunt. $25,000! That was more than enough money to save the farm and Hester and Issie both knew it. But her aunt wouldn't, she couldn't sell Comet. Could she?

Issie watched in horror as her aunt paused for a moment. Her face was expressionless as she looked at Issie. And then Hester reluctantly reached out a hand and took the cheque.

CHAPTER 17

Hester held the cheque in her hands and looked at it. Then she turned once more to the red-headed woman. "I'm sorry, Ginty. That's a lot of zeros you have written on here, but..."

Ginty looked Hester in the eye. "OK, Hester," she said. "If you want to play hardball. What do you want? Another $1,000? $2,000? All right, I'll make that a $28,000 cheque. I've got a client that this pony would be perfect for. She's looking for a new horse. And a horse just like this one could take her to the top." Ginty ran a hand down Comet's neck. "This pony will be perfect for Natasha."

Issie blinked. "You mean you're buying Comet for Natasha Tucker?"

Ginty looked taken aback. "You know Natasha?"

"We go to the same pony club," Issie said flatly.

"Well, she asked me to find her a new horse," Ginty said. "And I think I just have."

"Think again." Hester lifted up the cheque daintily between her fingers and ripped it carefully and cleanly in two.

"I'm sorry, Ginty, but I've been trying to tell you… Comet is not for sale. And even if he was for sale," she added, "you're talking to the wrong person. He doesn't belong to me."

Ginty stiffened. "Well, who is his owner then?"

"That would be my niece," Hester said, turning to Issie. "Comet's her pony, so Natasha will have the pleasure of seeing him at the next pony-club rally because Issie will be riding him there."

Issie was stunned. "Really? Aunty Hess, do you mean it? He's mine? To take back home with me and everything?"

"Absolutely!" Hester said. "That is, if you want him."

Issie didn't need any more convincing. "Of course I want him!" she said. She turned to Comet and threw her arms around his patchy chestnut and white neck.

"Well," Ginty sighed. "I think you're all mad, of

course. You won't get a price this good from anyone else in the business." She handed her card to Issie. "If you ever change your mind and want to sell him, these are my details. My offer still stands." Issie accepted the card and shoved it in her jodhpur pocket.

Ginty ran her eyes over Comet one last time. "That's quite the pony you have there," she said to Issie.

"I know," Issie replied. "He really is."

"Do you think we did the right thing?" Issie asked her aunt as they sat around the kitchen table back at Blackthorn Farm that evening. "I mean, should I have taken Ginty's money? It would have got you out of trouble – with the farm and everything, I mean."

Hester shrugged. "I suppose it would have been the logical thing to do," she said, "but then I was never really one for logic. Besides, I'm not sure that Comet would be worth all that money without you riding him. You and that skewbald were made for each other and I'm not about to split you up now. You've got a lot of adventures ahead of you yet. Maybe not at this farm – but I couldn't sell Comet to save this place. I just couldn't. Now,"

Hester looked around the table at Mrs Brown, Stella, Kate, Ben, Dan, Avery and Aidan, "shall I put the kettle on for tea then?"

Hester was just about to stand up when Issie shoved an envelope across the table to her. "Aunty Hess? I want you to have this."

Hester looked at the envelope in front of her on the table. She didn't pick it up.

"What is it?"

"$15,000," Issie said. "It's my winnings from the Puissance."

"Can I add something to that?" said a voice across the table. It was Aidan and he too thrust an envelope across the table at Hester. "It's $10,000. My winnings from the showjumping. I still came second in the novice hack – plus managed to ace a couple of other events on Destiny."

Aidan looked at Hester. "I want you to have the money. With my money and Issie's combined that makes $25,000. It's enough to save the farm for now. It will see us through until we get that next big film job."

Hester shook her head. "No. I won't let you kids do this. This is your money. I won't take your charity."

There was silence at the table – and then, finally, Mrs

Brown spoke. "I agree," she said. She turned to her sister, "You're right, Hess. I won't let Issie give you $15,000. That money could be her future. She could invest it and use it for university…"

"But, Mum! I want to do this…"

"Let me finish, Issie!" Mrs Brown said firmly. "I said I won't let you give it to your aunt, but I will let you invest it with her. That is, if Hester is willing to take you and Aidan on as her business partners." Mrs Brown smiled at her sister. "Hess, I know I always tease you about this place being a money pit, but since I got here I've been seeing things differently. It's beautiful here. I can see why you love it so much, and the riding school could be a real success in the future or maybe you could breed Blackthorn Ponies? If they all show as much promise as Comet then you could have a lucrative business on your hands selling up-and-coming showjumpers to people like Ginty McLintoch. Not to mention the film work, which I'm sure will pick up again."

Hester looked at her sister. "What exactly are you suggesting, Amanda?"

"I'm suggesting that you take Issie and Aidan on as your junior business partners."

Hester stared at the envelope on the table and then she picked it up and put it in her pocket. "Well," she said, extending a hand to an astonished Aidan and Issie, "I guess we should shake on that, don't you? I'm sure your mum can do some paperwork, Issie, and make it all official."

Aidan and Issie both took turns shaking her hand in stunned disbelief.

"Congratulations," Hester grinned at Issie. "You are now the proud owner of one skewbald gelding – and shareholder in an utterly barking mad horse farm!"

Leaving Blackthorn Farm was much harder this time. It wasn't just because it was Issie's farm too now. It was everything. The manor, the ponies, the kids...

"Even Kelly-Anne?" Stella had asked Issie teasingly.

"Well, maybe I won't miss Kelly-Anne," Issie said, "but even she hasn't been so bad lately."

In fact, since Stella had got Kelly-Anne to help out as groom at the Horse of the Year, there had been a real attitude change in her. On the last day of the riding school they had held a Blackthorn Farm Ribbon Day, and it was Kelly-Anne who had stayed up late the night before helping Issie, Stella and Kate to make homemade rosettes for all the riders.

There was a red rosette for first, blue for second and bright yellow for third place. Each rosette was made of ribbon with a round cardboard disc at the centre with *Blackthorn Farm Riding Club* written on it in scripty handwriting.

Issie, Stella and Kate were the judges for the Ribbon Day and they gave out prizes for loads of events. Kitty won most improved rider; Tina and Trisha won the prize on the palominos for the best dual jump. Sophie and Lucy had Molly and Pippen so shiny and well-plaited that they tied for first place in the best-groomed. George won the bending and Arthur won the flag race. Even Kelly-Anne joined in the competition in good spirits and won Best Rider over Hurdles, which she seemed to be completely thrilled about.

An official prize-giving was held on horseback at the end of the day and the rosettes were tied on to the ponies' bridles before all the riders did a victory lap together around the arena. Sophie was so thrilled with her yellow rosette that Issie noticed she was wearing it in her hair when she came to dinner that night.

Before they sat down to eat their dinner, the kids all raced off into the living room and returned with a cardboard box. "We've made prizes for all of you too," Sophie explained. From the box they produced a purple sash made out of crêpe paper for Kate that said Best Instructor. Stella got a homemade badge that said Most Fun Horsey Friend and Hester got one that said Favourite Holiday Organiser Ever.

"Well, they wouldn't give her one for her cooking, would they?" Stella whispered to Issie.

"We've got one for you too, Isadora," Kitty said. The kids gathered around the box and pulled out what looked like an old china teacup with a saucer underneath it. "It's a cup," Kitty said. "Well, I know it's only a teacup, but we thought it could be, like, a cup for winning the Puissance – and we've had it engraved and everything."

Issie looked at the teacup. It was cracked and it had a chip out of the saucer. "We found it in a pile of rubbish down by the stables," Kitty said. "It's not actually for you to drink out of or anything. It's to sit on your mantelpiece like a trophy."

"Thanks!" Issie smiled.

"Look at the engraving!" Lucy said.

Issie looked on the side of the teacup. The "engraving" was done in green felt tip. It said, *The Champion's Cup: awarded to Isadora Brown for Winning the Puissance and Saving Blackthorn Farm.*

Issie grinned. "Thanks, everyone – it's the best prize I've ever had."

The cup was placed alongside the other prizes in the centre of the table and Mrs Brown served up pizza and chips on to everyone's plates.

"I don't believe that this is our last dinner together before you all go home," Hester said. "It will be so quiet here when you are all gone. It's been so loud and full of life for the past few weeks. There's never been a quiet moment."

Actually, Issie thought, a quiet moment was exactly what she needed. A nice quiet moment when she could finally talk to Aidan about what had happened after Dan won the showjumping that day. She hadn't been able to talk to him when they were at the Horse of the Year. And then she was in Avery's truck sitting with her mum for the ride home. Since they'd been back at Blackthorn Farm it was just as Aunty Hess had said – there was never a quiet moment. It had been impossible to get some time alone with Aidan. Issie had finally resigned herself to the fact that she would never get a chance to tell Aidan how she felt. *Maybe that's a good thing*, she thought. If Aidan was really meant to be her boyfriend then wouldn't he have said something by now?

On their very last morning at the farm, Issie set her alarm clock for 5 a.m. It had become her ritual now, that every time she left this place she woke up before dawn and spent some time alone, feeding the animals breakfast, saying her own quiet goodbyes to all the horses before the rest of the world woke up and joined her.

When her alarm clock woke her up it was still pitch black outside, but by the time she was dressed and had pulled her farm boots on, the dawn light was already filtering through the trees on the horizon.

Down at the stables, Issie unbolted the stall doors one by one and watched as the horses all stuck their heads out to see who was there. Diablo stuck his head out first, and then Paris and Stardust.

"It's me," Issie whispered, moving down one side of the barn, feeding each of them in turn. "I've got carrots." At the mention of the word "carrot" there was a nicker from the first stall and Comet stuck his head over.

"Hey, boy," Issie grinned at him. "I'm taking you home today. You're coming to live with me. I can't wait for you to meet Blaze and Storm."

"So you're choosing him then?" Issie turned around to see Aidan standing behind her.

"Aidan!"

"I thought this was a competition between me and Dan," Aidan grinned at her, "but I can see now that the only one who's ever going to really win you over is Comet."

"No!" Issie felt her tummy somersaulting with nerves. "Aidan, that's what I've been trying to tell you, about the bet, the one you made with Dan…"

"It's OK," Aidan said, stepping closer to her. "I already know. I spoke to Dan and he told me what you said to him."

Issie was shocked. "You talked to Dan? When?"

"At the Horse of the Year," Aidan said. "I went to shake his hand and say congratulations on winning our bet and all that. He told me that the bet was off. He seemed to think that you wanted me to win…"

"I did… I mean, I do…" Issie was trembling as Aidan moved closer to her. Before she could say anything more he had put his arms around her and…

"Issie! There you are!" Avery's voice boomed through the stable.

Aidan jumped back at the sound of his voice, letting go of Issie. He tried to act casual. "I was, ummm, I was just feeding Comet a carrot…"

Avery raised an eyebrow at him. "Come on, you two!" he said briskly. "Breakfast is ready and Hester asked me to come and get you. We don't have much time. I want to be packed and out of here by 9 a.m. It's a long drive back to Chevalier Point with five horses in the truck."

Issie and Aidan both hesitated, hoping that Avery would walk on ahead and leave them alone again for a moment, but the instructor stood at the door waiting to escort them back to the manor.

"Well? Come on? What are you waiting for?"

The rest of the morning was much the same. "It's a big farm," Issie grumbled to Stella and Kate. "You'd think there'd be enough room for me to be alone with my boyfriend for five minutes."

"Boyfriend?" Stella's ears pricked up. "Issie, is Aidan really, finally, your boyfriend?"

Issie shrugged. "I don't know. I guess so."

"I thought he was your business partner," Kate grinned.

"That too," Issie grinned back.

It was a departure on a grand scale that day. Aidan was driving Hester's horse truck with all the kids in it to take them back to their homes now the camp was over. And Avery, Mrs Brown and the Chevalier Point gang were going home together in Avery's truck at the same time.

"That's the last of it," Issie said as she threw a sleeping bag into the storage box in the back of the horse truck. "You can bring the horses on now."

As Dan and Aidan walked Madonna and Max up the truck ramp, Issie, Stella and Kate went to get Toby, Coco and Comet.

Issie looked around the stables longingly one last time. She had almost kissed Aidan here this morning. She had been hoping that she might see him here again and get the chance to say goodbye, but it looked like there was no hope.

"Come on, Comet," she said as she led the skewbald out of his stall. "It's time for us to go home."

The horses were loaded, and so were the kids. Aunt Hester had handed everyone bundles of inedible jam scones to see them through the long drive through the Gisborne gorge, and they were all ready to go home.

"Right," Avery said. "Are we all onboard and ready?"

Issie jumped up into the cab next to Avery and did up her seatbelt. "Uh-huh. Everyone is in their seats. We're ready to…" There was a loud tapping on the driver's window. It was Aidan.

Avery wound his window down. "What is it?" he said. "We need to get going; we've got the horses onboard."

Aidan took a deep breath. "I know that, sir. It's just that I need to talk to Issie for a moment. It's something I wanted to say to her earlier, but we got interrupted and, well, I really need to talk to her."

Avery looked annoyed by this, but he turned to Issie. "Aidan's got something he wants to talk about, apparently. You've got one minute."

Issie leapt down out of the cab and Aidan grabbed her by the hand and dragged her back across the lawn so that they were standing a few metres away from the trucks underneath the falling petals of the cherry trees.

"Listen, Issie, about before," he said. "I never finished saying what I wanted to say and, well, I wanted to let you know that… I hope you'll be…" He stopped talking and looked up. Peering out of the two horse trucks were a dozen faces, all pressed up against the glass, watching them.

"Oh, great!" Aidan groaned. "Just what I needed. An audience!" He looked back at Issie. "I'm not going to talk about this any more," he said. "You know what I mean and you know what I'm trying to say. Now this is it. I don't care any more. I'm going to kiss you, OK?"

"But, Aidan!" Issie objected. "I can't. They're all watching us!"

Aidan smiled and pulled her closer. "Close your eyes then," he told her.

And she did.